All the Way Home

Way Home Series Book One

By

Kim Mills

All The Way Home

Copyright © 2017 Kim Mills
All Rights Reserved

Front cover designed by lisabook

Editing by Susan Soares: SJS Editorial Services

Illustrations by Dh
(There are no illustrations)

Contents

Acknowledgements

I am here but by the grace of my God, and forever grateful that His mercies are new each morning because I never fail to need them.

To my husband, it's been 22 years, give or take a month, and you still give me goosebumps. Thank you for every time you quieted the defeated voice in my head that wanted to give up and replaced it with your voice encouraging me to keep at it. Freckles, Drama and Monster; I know there are days I disappeared in front of the computer. Thanks for still thinking I'm the best mom ever, even when you have to make your own dinner.

For everyone that reads *She is Fierce*. The blog, the articles, the travel, the book.... It's all yours. It amazes me every single day that you are all following along on this journey. My story is your story. Thank you for your support, and for those times you trust me with your voice.

For my Beta Reader group, thank you for your encouragement, your criticisms, your honesty and your time. You're the best.

I'm an armoured soldier's spouse who wrote a book about a fictional infantryman. So for every time Dh answered my infantry questions with "I don't know, *Kim*, why don't you ask a *Patricia*," I give a big thank you to all our Dirty Patricia friends who were willing to take my calls. To all our military family who has answered my questions and put up with my writing over the years, I am showing my appreciation the way I know you'd want it: By keeping your damn name out of it.

What can I say? I'm high maintenance. Everything I've done has taken a village. So for everyone that's been a part of that village throughout our journey, thank you.

This book is dedicated to Dh.

For that time when we were 18 and you marched me into the bank with you and signed papers to make all that was yours, ours. This is me doing the same thing, 17 years later.

Who I am and what I accomplish cannot be separated from who you are and what you give me.

This has always been for you.

That's why God made love so strong, so it could carry us all the way home.

~ Franklin P. Jones

One

1999

Juliette

The first time I see him I feel nothing special.

To be fair, I've felt a lot of nothing for a long time. Walking home from work at one a.m., I'm confident on the streets of my suburban neighbourhood from the sheer knowledge that the only ones up to no good here are my friends. It isn't uncommon for a car to pull up or a group to emerge from a parking lot or back alley and see me, calling out my name and urging me to join them. Right now, though, even if it's Saturday night and early by my usual standards, I have a good forty-five-minute walk ahead of me and after the night at work, I just want to get home.

I pull my fingers from the cuffs of my long-sleeved shirt and grab a cigarette from my purse, stopping for just a second to turn my back to the wind and light it. There had been a time when I'd have stuck to the back roads to smoke so no one would see me and tell my parents, but at this time of night, my parents are long in bed and the neighbours have given up trying to warn them about me. My headphones blare Green Day in my ears and soon I walk with a mission. I shut out the world, the night spent waiting tables for families who didn't notice me, the ache in my heels from being on my feet for eight hours. I focus on the hot bath I can take at home and the lure of sleeping in until noon.

When he pulls up behind me, I really don't notice. I remember being taught ever since I was little to walk with a purpose. Shoulders back, eyes front. Always make them think you have somewhere to be and someone waiting for you there. My parents aren't much for the after-school-special type life lessons, but that was one thing they made sure I learned early. I always walk like that now out of habit, usually flicking my favourite lighter, a stainless-steel Bic with an engraved picture of Betty Boop on the front, around in my hand. I love it, even if I can't remember the name of the guy who gave it to me. The lighter stuck, even if he didn't. I don't even think we dated a month.

I like to call it dating. Dating is what teenagers do, right? Besides, that makes it sound more romantic than what it almost always is.

The biker's presence only registers because the engine drowns out the music in my ears, but still I resist turning to look at whoever pulled up behind me. I think maybe he's pulling into the house behind me, stopping to look at directions, anything that means he isn't pulling over to talk to me. Without looking down, I think over the clothes I threw on this afternoon before I headed out to start my shift. Hip-hugger jeans, a halter top with an open sweater over it and worn-down heeled sandals. I'm just five foot one at seventeen years old; I've seemed small compared to my peers for a few years already. I'm also softer than I wish I was. The outline of my black bra can be seen as it stretches the logo on my cream-coloured top. My streaked hair is falling out of the ponytail that holds it half up, I'm sure my makeup is faded to nothing. There's nothing about me that would make a stranger stop to notice.

I hear the engine turn off and suddenly Welcome to Paradise fills my ears again. I'd figured the rider had gone into one of the houses, so I'm caught off guard when I feel his hand at the small of my back.

"What the hell!" I spin around into him, my hip bone crashing into the helmet he holds in his hands. It's instinct for me to step back to look up at his face. He grabs my wrist as though he thinks I'm going to take off, but he doesn't need to. I'm not someone who runs. Even if I was, not in these shoes.

"Whoa, hey, relax. I'm not going to hurt you." He lets go when he realizes I'm not going anywhere and I stare at him.

He's beautiful. I don't know if beautiful is the right word, but it's the first thing I think of. I'd assumed he'd be older, I don't know why. I guess I don't know many teenagers with motorcycles, but he looks my age. His hair is soft brown and sticking up all over his head, damp with sweat from his helmet, and with the streetlight at his back, there is almost a copper colour on the tips. He has green eyes. It strikes me that they're looking at me with more intensity than I think this little encounter requires. There is a dusting of freckles on his face and down his neck that leads to big shoulders. In fact, all of him is bulky—not fat, far from soft, just... big. I bet if someone stood on the other side of him, it'd look like I'd disappeared behind him. I can still feel where his hand had touched my back.

He walks back to his bike and I stand there, watching like an idiot, still trying to figure out what is happening. He unclips a helmet from his backpack and tosses it at me. I'm amazed I catch it even though I'm completely confused. It's heavy and bulky. The black on the sides is worn through to the silver underneath and the strap is frayed.

"It's a good thing you're in jeans. Where do you live? I'm giving you a ride home. You *are* going home, right?"

I think I'll say something, but then close my mouth and pull out my ponytail so I can get the helmet on. The thought occurs to me that even strangers can tell what I am now: a girl who doesn't really know how to say no.

"Shit, girl. Really? My name is Tavish, by the way. I didn't expect you to get on my bike without even asking my name." He sounds annoyed, but the way he's looking at me is more protective than pissed off. I'm not sure who he thinks he's protecting me from; there are few people on these streets I don't know. He's the stranger here. Besides, as sad as it is at seventeen, something I've learned over and over already is that no one can take anything if you give it all away.

"If you tell me your name, I'm expected to remember it in the morning." I've repeated this line more than a few times. I let myself flash the same suggestive smile I swear I could give in my sleep. I'm tired and not going to turn down a quick trip home.

"You'll remember it." He speaks without moving his jaw. I cock my head and look a little closer at him. His eyes are piercing, and he's clenching and unclenching his fists at his side. It doesn't seem intimidating, though, more like a nervous habit. The motion is at odds with the rest of his confidence, but he's not following where my suggestive tone is leading and that's unusual. I'm not sure what to make of him but I'm too tired to care.

"Well, if I have to, you have to. I'm Juliette," I say, as I put my hand on his shoulder and hop up onto the bike behind him. I'm used to motorcycles. My dad and his friends are all riders and I've been on them since I was a kid. I never liked speed bikes though, because they're not designed to hold another person. I slide right against him instantly and have to brace myself so I don't bump his helmet with mine. I put my arms around his waist; he sits there for a moment. He smells a little like leather from his jacket, with almost a pine scent underneath. It's comforting, and I have an unusual urge to try to reach my head closer to breathe him in. Thankfully, the bulk of the helmet forces me to keep my head back and stops me from attempting anything embarrassing.

"So... you just want to hang out back there or are you going to tell me where we're headed?"

"I'll tell you where to turn, Slick. You just drive."

He shakes his head and starts the bike, pulling back onto the road. "Your parents going to care if I drop you off on this?" he yells back to me over the growl of the engine.

"On a bike? No. On *this* bike? Maybe. But they're fast asleep, don't worry about it."

"Too fast for them?" he asks and I snicker. Like that would be the problem. My safety isn't their concern, just their image.

"They're more Harley than Kawasaki, that's all," I say. He nods like that makes sense. He's clearly been down this road before. Even without being a rider myself, I knew just from being around my dad that the kinds of people who like motorbikes are usually snarky about the kind of bike they prefer.

"Me too, but you take what you can get." That surprises me. Really, everything about this guy seems to and it's only been five minutes.

When we get to my place, I hop off. He kicks down the stand and rises, his big frame leaning against his bike while I take off my helmet and hand it to him. As he straightens from attaching the helmet back to his bag, I put myself right next to him, probably too close if it weren't for the fact that I'm sure I know what he's looking for. It's always the same thing, no matter what they say.

"You going to give me your number?" he breathes down near my ear, making no move to take advantage.

"Sure, if that's what you want," I say, and I grab a scrap of a receipt from my purse, press it against his chest and pull out a pen to write it down. He looks down and grabs something else from my purse. A graffiti marker.

"Hey!" I snap, but as soon as he stuffs the paper with my number in his pocket he takes hold of my wrist in one hand and pulls the cap off with his teeth. Then he writes on my arm in big black letters. I giggle, figuring that's probably the right answer. It usually is. When he lets go, I step closer to him and reach my face up, dusting my lips across his neck. His hand grips my hips for a moment, seeming almost unsure, so I press them into him. I can feel him hard against my stomach.

"You don't have to do this," he whispers in my ear. Before I can ask, he turns and straddles his bike. "I'll call you." He says it like he's a little unsure, but then nods to my arm. "That's in case you think of getting on someone else's bike without even asking their name. Next time, you call me."

And he's gone.

I look down at the scrawling black letters that are slowly blurring as the ink bleeds into my skin.

SHE ALREADY HAS A RIDE HOME.

***

He calls before I even get out of the bath.

"Hey," he says. He still sounds confident, but I can swear underneath he's almost shaky. Is he nervous? That doesn't make sense. I'm not the kind of girl that guys get nervous around.

"Hey there, Slick," I say. He scoffs into the phone but doesn't argue. I think I like his new nickname.

"Still up? What are you doing?"

"I'm in the bath," I answer and smile when I hear the faintest groan. Maybe he's interested after all. "Hold on, I'm drying off to get into bed."

Once I'm tucked in, we start talking. He's at a different high school than me, we are both in our last year. He's an only child. I guess his dad was in the Army but Tavish has never met him. When his mom got pregnant, they barely knew each other. They were still in their teens and he was a recruit she met at a bar, so she never told him. She just quietly moved back in with her parents in another province. She works at Tavish's school in the office but he doesn't live with her; he lives with his grandparents. I guess her current boyfriend doesn't want him around, which sounds awful but Tavish doesn't seem to care. He has a job at a warehouse stocking shelves on weeknights. He likes to draw and he plays on the football team, which seems like a weird combination. Turns out one of his teammates lives in my neighbourhood, which is where he was when he saw me.

"What about you?" he asks when I can't think of any more questions to keep the focus off me. "Who are you?"

"My dad is a bus driver and my mom is a hairdresser. I have an older sister, but she's already moved away for college and I doubt she'll be back. I don't have any artistic talents, but I do love music. I work part time at Smitty's waiting tables. There's not much to me."

"Bullshit. I'm gonna figure you out."

I don't know how to answer that, so we are quiet for a minute. Then he asks me something about a concert I attended and we end up talking until I can see the sky redden out my window. No one has ever stayed up talking with me like this and when I realize what's happened, I panic a little about where this leads. I decide to bring it back to what I know.

"Well, Slick, you still managed to keep me up all night," I purr. "It's too bad it was just over the phone or I could've thanked you for the ride with a little more fun. I still can, anytime. I promise I'll make it worth it."

I hear Tavish grind his teeth before he answers, "Do you always do that?"

"Do what?"

"Assume you have to give it up like that."

I bite my lip. Maybe I'm exhausted; I don't know why I answer honestly. "It's what I'm good at." I try to lighten the mood. "Next time I see you, I'll show you what I mean." I can't tell him everything. He doesn't need to know all I've done, *everyone* I've done. I'm sure once he asks the right people, he'll find out soon enough. When that happens, he'll either want nothing to do with me or he'll want *everything* to do with me. That's how this works. That's how it always works.

"You don't have to do that with me. You don't have to be this girl, you know. I'll keep calling you even if you're not."

I sigh. "You know how in movies and books and on TV, there's always characters that have these amazing guy friends. They don't want to date them, or fuck them. Instead, they're just protective over them, like a big brother. They just want to hang out and get coffee and they do favours for each other," I pause, "like drive each other home." I'm letting this get too complicated, but for some reason I keep talking.

"I always thought that would be amazing, you know, to have that. I always wanted a friend like that..." I don't know how to explain the next part. "But that's not how real life works. Guys don't want to be your friend, even when they say they do. At least, they don't want to be *my* friend. They always eventually want something more from me, and after that, I'm not their friend. I'm just that girl they messed around with. It's so much easier to just start there, so I know where I stand."

The truth is if I really think about it, it hasn't been that long since I'd given up on more. One'd think at seventeen I'd still be holding out for romance but I've never found that and it already hurts less not to try. It is easy to end up here; it only takes one time, one mistake, to start down this path. Once I'm here, no one ever sees me differently. There's no point in regrets—I am who I am—and it's no one's fault but my own.

"You always have a choice to be this girl," he whispers, and it gets my back up. He doesn't get it.

"I think I only really had the choice the first time."

There's a long silence. I immediately regret my honesty.

"It's not a big deal, Tavish, it's okay. I just thought you—"

"Stop." His voice is strained. "Don't. I can do that, Juliette." For a second, I almost think it sounds like he's convincing himself, but when he speaks again, he sounds certain. "That friends thing? I can do that. I can be that friend. That's what we're going to have, you and me, okay? I promise."

"Wow. I must really not be your type," I mutter a little nervously. Tavish growls.

"You've no idea what my type is. I'd just rather be your friend than someone you fuck because you think that's what you're supposed to do, and then you try to forget about the next day. I don't want to be your one-night mistake, so I'm going to be your friend."

I'm not convinced, but I guess we'll see.

Two

Tavish

I have no idea what possesses me to stop.

That's a lie. I know why I do. The girl is fucking gorgeous. I'd just pulled out from my buddy's house, and I can see her walking down the street. The car behind me at the corner ends up driving around me before I realize I've been staring at her for so long I've forgotten to turn. She's wearing these skin-tight jeans and a long plaid shirt. I can only see her back, and I'm still mesmerized by her: straight blond hair streaked with dark colour, up in a half ponytail that bounces as she walks in these ridiculous sandals that are clearly not intended for any kind of distance, no matter how comfortable she seems in them. I can tell even from here she's short, and she's walking like she's in a hurry. I glance at my watch. A girl looking like that shouldn't be walking alone in a shitty neighbourhood like this by herself at this time of night.

When I get close to her and she turns around, for a moment I can't breathe. Even though her hair looks naturally blonde, her eyes are soft brown. The contrast manages to look somehow gentle. Her face is heart shaped, and she has soft, rounded cheekbones. Her nose, left eyebrow and bottom lip are pierced. That lip... I stare at her lips for at least a moment too long. They're perfect.

I really don't expect her to get on my bike. I don't know what I was going to do if she didn't. That's a lie. I'd have walked with her. But she just hops on, without a care in the world, and lets me drive her to her house.

Even more unexpectedly, as soon as we park at her parents' place, she comes on to me. I want to believe it's me, but I could see in her eyes that she's just going through the motions. She thinks she has to, as what, some kind of payment? When she grinds her hips on me, I can't hide my excitement, but the whole taking advantage thing just isn't me. I desperately wish it was, but it's just not. As much as I want to, and I really, really want to, I can't do it. For reasons I can't even explain, instead of following my hormones and jumping on the chance with the beautiful girl who is obviously willing to thank me for the ride, I shut her down.

I don't have a clue why I have this burning need to get to know Juliette. I do, however, have a feeling that taking her as far as I could in her parents' driveway won't be the first step in getting her to open up. Defying every teenage dream screaming in my ears to shut up and go with it, to grab her by the hips and find somewhere to take it to the next level, I get her number and put some distance between the two of us while I still have some resolve.

I know I'll call right away, just as much as I know it makes me look like a pussy. I need to talk to her, and lying in my own bed, with her on the phone, is a much safer distance to learn who she is. As it turns out, she's just as gorgeous as she looks. No one has ever been as excited about my art as my football game, but Juliette wants to hear all about it. She even listens without laughing when I tell her about joining the Army when I graduate. Besides my grandparents, everyone always assumes it's some little boy dream, like a toddler telling everyone they want to be a superhero when they grow up, but it's not. It's who I know I'm supposed to be and she seems to accept that without question. For some reason, I even tell her the messed-up story about my mom and I never talk about that to anyone. It's not like I'm the only kid who never met their deadbeat dad, or whose mom wishes he'd never come around to mess up her life. All in all, with Gran and Gramps around for me, I've had it pretty good.

Her story is different but I don't know if it hurts less. Her parents are still married but according to her, they are miserable.

Juliette is sure they're still together for her sake, and it sounds like they make that clear to her all too often. From what she tells me, her parents like to sound strict, but they also like to keep their heads in the sand. They refuse to believe what she's up to, preferring instead to let her say whatever she wants as long as it sounds good. I can relate to a life more concerned with what people think instead of what really happens.

She makes me laugh and somehow, we forget the time. She makes me forget everything that isn't right there in the words between us. She captivates me with the way she says my name, the way she giggles at my jokes, the way she shares her life and gets me to share mine.

As we talk, I absentmindedly sketch, desperate to never forget, even for a minute, how she looked on the back of my bike, how she looked walking up to her front door, how she looked pressed against me. By the time I even realize I've been doing it, I have a pile of pencil drawings around my bed and they're all of her.

As beautiful as she sounds as we talk, she also sounds broken. I can tell when she talks about her friends that none of them really care about her, and she knows it. She talks a lot about "girls like her," and I wonder how many times other people have told her who she is. I feel the instant my heart makes the irrational decision to spend my life helping her see who she is under all the lies she's believed.

By the time morning comes, we've been talking for hours. Suddenly, I feel her slip back into that part she seems to play. I think it's what she does when she's nervous or doesn't know what to say, and I hate it. I don't have to even see her face to know that she shuts herself down when she goes there. It's like a coping mechanism. For whatever reason, instead of doing what it should and making me want to take full advantage of what she's offering, it leaves me with a burning need to protect her. It's only been one night, but I'm even more sure now that I want the real Juliette. I want to see her face when she really wants me, and not just because it's easy for her. I want to be the one she drops the act for. Even I can't believe it, but I'm sacrificing all she'd give me right now for the chance to one day be the one she can give everything to.

When we get to saying goodbye, I realize there's only one way to do that. I need to promise to be something she's never had before: a friend who won't try to be anything more. It's the first time I've ever made a promise I'm one hundred percent sure I'll break. I'm just hoping that when I do, she'll forgive me.

***

This week at school I ask around about her. I don't go to the same school, so it seems that while most of the other kids I ask know of her, no one really has anything insightful. They know the group she hangs out with, the guys she's been with. I make the mistake of asking the guys about her after football practice too.

"Wait, the blonde? Short girl, big tits, lip ring? Yeah. I *know* her." Shane, our quarterback, smirks. "She was at that party over in Bowness over the summer. That chick didn't even know her own name by the time I got with her. I don't even know if I was the first. You know, *that night*. Not bad, though, why? You fuck her?"

All the blood rushes past my ears at once. "Are you kidding me, Shane? That's okay now, banging girls when they're too drunk to even know what's happening? What the hell?" The rest of the change room looks at me like I've lost my mind as I stand inches from Shane's face. I'm bigger than he is; I know I can take him. The rest of the team, though… That's not going to work out for me. I try to think clearly before I get myself killed over a girl I just met.

Shane just laughs, though. "Girls like that, Tavish, it's just fucking implied, man. Besides, she didn't say no." He gives me a sick look. "That girl always wants it. That's why she's there. Like I said, I doubt I was even the first that night, so if you did get a piece, I hope you at least wrapped it up."

It's all I can do not to punch him out, but standing here in a towel with the entire team looking on isn't the time. I reassure myself that I can just let him take a tackle next game. Did I not block that? Oops. So, I shrug it off and shake my head, going back to getting dressed. I yank my jeans on quickly since the conversation has turned to whether any of the rest of them have been with her (thankfully no), which then leads them to "girls like her." I'm really starting to hate that phrase. I can't decide if I'm angrier at them for assuming, or her for giving up. I keep reminding myself that she's not mine to defend.

I decide to give myself time before I call her again. If this is a friendship, then I'm going to have to act like it; calling every night isn't going to make that happen. I wait a week or so. It's late again, and I'm just getting off work stocking shelves when I call her from the office. She says she's at the train station. I ask her when the last bus runs to her place from there and her answer isn't entirely coherent. Something about being sure she'll find *someone* at the station willing to drive her home. I tell her to wait there and I'll come get her. I slam down the phone, barely noticing when it doesn't even stay on the hanger before I'm out the door. Damn it! How often does she do this?

By the time I pull up at the station, she's sitting cross-legged on a bench, smoking, talking to a couple greasy looking guys who are not even hiding how they're crudely undressing her with their eyes. Not that it'd be much of a stretch, because her shirt is hardly covering even the bare minimum. She's flicking that lighter again. I noticed she was doing that the first night I saw her. I'm sure it's a nervous habit, and I wonder how long these jerks have been chatting her up. She jumps up when I pull up on the bike, and man, that shirt wasn't built to hold her while she skips over. Suddenly, the way I'm sitting on this bike is awfully uncomfortable. She unhooks the helmet from the bag on the back and smiles at me when she puts it on. She smells like cheap liquor, pot and cigarettes, but her pupils are almost entirely concealing the brown in her eyes—that's not all she's had tonight.

"Who's that?" I motion to the two guys who are still smoking by the bench, smirking at me. It occurs to me they were probably trying to get her to go back to wherever they're heading, and what they're smoking was most likely meant to help with that. Well, assholes, helps to have a motorcycle, doesn't it? No one wants to take the bus. As soon as she's distracted with jumping on the bike, I change the look I'm giving them, sit all the way up and glare at them in a way that in no uncertain terms tells them to fuck off and has them quickly moving along.

"Huh? Oh, I dunno. I think they go to my school?" She slides in behind me and doesn't even hesitate to snake her arms around my waist until her hands press against my stomach, just above my belt. I know I'm in good shape, but when I hunch forward in my seat to start riding, her hands make me regret every time in my life I've skipped the gym.

I have no idea where I'm taking her, but I don't want to bring her home yet. We drive and drive until we end up at a Denny's, where I convince her to come in and let me buy her a coffee and something to eat. I know this kind of familiarity is unexpected for her, but the way she slowly opens up at the table until she's talking and giggling, asking me to explain football with salt and pepper shakers, almost breaks my heart. The girl is so strong, far stronger than she thinks she is and really, really good at faking sober, but I can tell after a couple hours when her hands stop trembling and her eyes look less wild that she's finally coming down. It's after two before her eyelids start to droop lower, her movements slow and she shows signs of being tired. I wonder how long she's been awake but I'm scared to ask. I don't think it's just one night.

"You must be exhausted, Jules; let me take you home."

She reaches over and takes my hand. "I know I'm no fun sober, Slick, but... can we stay a little while longer? This part is the hardest." Her eyes plead, and she almost looks scared.

"You know, Juliette, the only reason I stuck around with you high like that is because I wanted the chance to spend more time with you sober. Not the other way around. We don't have to go anywhere as long as you stay awake enough to ride on the back of the bike."

She blinks hard. I think she might cry. I don't know how often I'll be amazed that no one has ever told her these things before. How her spirit has already ended up so damaged at seventeen. "That's not true," she whispers to the table. "Everyone says how I'm more fun, more energetic, more... I'm just *more* when I'm... when I'm not sober. When I'm sober, I'm no fun to be around."

"I'm not everyone, Jules. You were sober when I met you and I thought you were great. I'll always love hanging out with you, but I think you're amazing when you're just you. You don't need all that crap to be fun."

"Do you? I like you like this, right now, but I guess I never really thought about the fact that you never talk about partying. I realize we don't have the same friends or groups or whatever, but don't you ever just want to let go?"

I'm not sure what it is about her that makes me give her answers I don't give anyone else. "Not really. I mean, I drink sometimes when I'm out with friends. I guess I just don't like feeling out of control."

Juliette looks up from the table wistfully. "I think that's why I do, because I *want* to feel out of control. Like nothing is really happening, you know? Like none of it's really me and there's no consequences."

Soon after that she dozes off, leaning against the window. I could wake her and take her home, but I let her sit for a while. Instead, I grab the marker sticking out of the side of her purse, and I draw her on the napkin: hair hanging in her face with a strand stuck to her lip gloss, the charm from the choker around her neck nestled in the dip of her throat, my sweater hanging off her shoulders. When I'm done, I leave it there, half under my plate, and brush the hair from her face to wake her. She stirs, and I let her know I'm going to pay the bill. She starts to get her things to head out with me.

By the time I take her home, it's almost four, and she's shaking a little when she steps off my bike. I grab onto her for a second and just hold her while she trembles. It's not at all cold.

"Breathe, Jules." I press her head against my chest, and I close my eyes, focusing on my own breathing and feeling her slow herself to the sound of my heartbeat and the rise and fall of my chest. "Good girl. Just breathe."

Eventually, I watch from my bike until I see her step safely into her house. A couple weeks ago, I said I'd be her friend because

I didn't want to break her, but I'm sure she's going to be the one to break me.

Three

2001

Juliette

I feel a little more grown up now, but if I'm honest, I know life hasn't really changed since graduation last year. It's one a.m. on Saturday night, and instead of some shitty family restaurant, I'm walking out of some shitty bar. Instead of a part time job for spending money I actually have to pay bills. The rest isn't all that different. I plug in my headphones, trying to block out the sound of someone throwing up in the parking lot, the drunk adults I served who don't notice me past my boobs and the ache in my feet from standing behind a beer tub for six hours. My phone rings as I cross the street.

"Hey." His voice is familiar now. Sometimes it's days between calls, sometimes it's months. He shows up now and then to drive me home. When I really think about it, it's always those times when I'm in the worst place that he's there. He rarely asks questions, even when I'm clearly wearing yesterday's clothes and makeup, even when I'm slumped over against the fence in the park or the booth at the bar, drunk or high or both, in no condition to go anywhere after all my "friends" have scattered. Each time he looks a little less hopeful, but he never asks questions.

Sometimes when he calls, I can't hear him over the music and the crowd. Other times, we talk my whole walk home. There are times I've come to in the morning with my phone under my face, the indents almost painful on my skin. I think it's those times, when I'm in my room, terrified of the demons scratching my skin, that I'm the one who calls him. I don't even remember those calls, just the sleepy sound of his voice in the morning, telling me it's okay and I can hang up now and get some rest. I think, *I know*, those are the times I just don't want to be alone.

"Hey, I'm just getting off work. How was your night?" I hear him let out a breath. I know he's happiest when he catches me after work because I'm usually sober and alone. He's still the only one I know who prefers me that way.

"Can I drive you home?" He sounds... resigned? Worried?

"You don't have to. I'm almost at the train."

"I know." When I look up, he's right there across the street.

"Hey, stranger," I call to him, putting my phone back in my purse, my steps lighter walking over to him.

"You walked right by me," he glares. "It's scary how little you notice your surroundings."

"Sorry, Slick." I give him a quick hug. I don't know why that name sticks, but it does. Probably because the better I know him, the more I realize how out of character his behaviour had been that first night. Tavish doesn't pick up strange girls on the side of the road. He barely picks up girls he knows.

He's constantly on my case to be safe. I've never understood what he thinks is so valuable about me that I need to forever be on guard. He thinks I don't see the way he looks at the people with me when he picks me up on his bike. I wonder if maybe he doesn't even realize he does it anymore. He was never a small guy, even when we were younger, but he's grown bigger and he's more than just strength. He's fierce. To everyone else, he can look intimidating. To me, he's still just Slick. He should be too good of a friend to know there's nothing about me worth stealing.

He tosses me the helmet, and we walk back to his bike in silence. It may be summer, but the chill hasn't left the nights and it's still a little cold to ride a motorcycle after dark on the Canadian prairies. I don't know if there are many days of the year here that it's not, but the bike is the one thing he owns and Tavish hates borrowing his grandparents' car. He pulls a pair of his sweatpants out of his backpack and holds them out to me. Suddenly, I'm painfully aware I'm wearing a button-down halter top and jean shorts with the pockets sticking out the bottom. He never lets me ride with bare legs, but he always has something for me to wear in that bag. I take the pants and pull them on as he shrugs out of his jacket and throws it around my shoulders. He's just wearing a t-shirt underneath, and I see an old-school style tattoo on his forearm, still raised and pink.

"Tavish Cleary!" I exclaim and grab his wrist. I've gotten more than a little ink over the past year, but he hadn't had any the last time I saw him. Had it been that long? I tried to think back. It had been probably a month or more since the last time he picked me up. He grins but pulls away, grabbing a wind jacket from his bag and putting it on.

"Later. I'll show you later," he mumbles.

We pull onto the road. I relax and lean into him as he weaves through traffic and drives outside the city. We never just go home. Suddenly, he turns off the highway and onto a dirt road, stopping at a cement shell of a graffiti-covered building that used to be a roadside gas station.

I jump off, take off my helmet and look at him, but he just grins and pulls me to the other side of the cement wall. At some point, others left logs and chairs here, probably for some bush party. He sits and I pull out a cigarette. We sit in silence for a long while, the highway trucks passing loudly, and every once in a while, I can hear a pack of coyotes in the distance. The only light is the muted street lights from the highway and the glow of my smoke.

"I'm leaving for Basic Training tomorrow."

This shouldn't be a surprise. I know he'd applied. Hell, I've known since that first night this is what he wants to do. I feel like we've been talking about it forever. It's one of those things that is going to happen. One day. I knew this was coming. I mean, I guess I knew.

I didn't really know.

My first thought is to yell at him to stay, but when my voice comes out, it's strangely quiet. "Okay." It amazes me how many times Tavish has left me without the slightest idea what the right response is. What do you say to someone when following their dream means they will leave you behind?

We are quiet again. He looks almost defeated, so I put out my cigarette and sit next to him. "You don't have to do this, you know." I say it because I want him to remember why he's going to do it anyway. I already know his response before he opens his mouth.

"Yes, I do. It's what I want. It's what I've always wanted. It's... it's who I am. If it wasn't, I'd never leave." It's the last sentence that seems to hurt him.

"We are all going to leave, Slick. I think it's amazing that you found what you want in life. You're going to be phenomenal at it. I'm sure of it."

He's very still, looking at me. Then he rips off his jacket and spreads in on the floor, pulling me down to lay beside him. We look up through the roofless building to the prairie sky. Eventually, I ask him questions: where is he going, how long will he be at each place, what will his job be like? We talk almost in whispers to each other until he pulls me up and around the corner, where we can watch the sunrise over the canola fields. When the sky is almost entirely lit up, he says, "I'm going to break a promise and you might never forgive me."

I have no idea what he's talking about, but exhaustion has kicked in and I look over through heavy lids at his face. Have I ever noticed the green of his eyes before? It's not just like the green I see anywhere else. It's more like a liquid, like photos of the ocean that I see in vacation ads. I'm too busy figuring that out to prepare myself. His lips brush right on top of mine, and he whispers, "I'm so sorry, I tried."

When he kisses me, he's not sorry. He's fierce. Possessive. We had both slumped down against the wall, watching the sun, but he's up on his knees next to me now, one hand holding my face up to his and the other in my hair. I lift my hand and, not knowing what to do with it, I place it on his bicep. Has he always been this strong? He moves closer and his knee presses between my legs. I push up against him and drop my hand to the front of his jeans, but he backs off. I shiver, feeling the loss of his body covering me.

He drops his face down level with mine and searches my eyes. I'm still in shock so I give him my best seductive grin. He closes his eyes and sits back, away from me.

"FUCK!" he spits out through clenched jaw. "I broke my promise and I fucked this up."

I'm just gaping at him, confused. Did he not want to kiss me? I mean, he's leaving in a matter of hours, so it makes sense that he could use that kind of friend tonight. We've spent a lot of time together in the past two years and he's never made a move— not that I haven't wanted him to. I've never let myself want it. Tavish has always been too good for me that way. He dates pretty girls he can take on his arm, girls whose names have never been written on bathroom walls. I accepted long ago he'd never want that from me so I've just focused on being grateful for his friendship and I've never let my heart even try.

Maybe he is looking for comfort tonight, and he knows I can do that. Am I so far from his type that he doesn't even want me when he's spending the next few months going without?

"I promised you we could be friends, Juliette. I said I could and I have, because I wanted you to have that. To have someone you can call when you're scared or tired or need a favour. To have a protector and confidant just like you wanted. And you do! I am that! I knew I'd want more, I knew it, but I thought if I waited long enough, you could give it to me and know you'd still always have that first part, no matter what. I wanted to wait until we could do this," he motions frantically between us, "without you turning into the girl who thinks she has no choice. But I'm leaving and so I rushed it and I didn't wait long enough. I can see it. As soon as I kiss you, you give me that smile and that look in your eyes, and I know it's the same look you've given every other douchebag who's ever taken from you. I won't be him. Until you know I'm not him, until you can do this without finding that place in you that shuts off your heart, we're not doing this."

I'm still staring at him with my mouth open. He's quieter now, "If we do this now, you'll stop thinking you ever had that movie-style friendship and think that you're just that girl I messed around with. You'll never be that girl to me, no matter what. I don't want to leave if you doubt that. So, we can't. I can't. Let's go back to five minutes ago, and pretend I never screwed this up and I never kissed you. Okay?"

I don't understand but I just nod. It's late and I don't want to mess up our last night together.

By the time we stand up off the cold dirt, the rush hour traffic crawls into the city. Just before he pulls his jacket up off the ground, I catch his new tattoo in the light for the first time.

It's a motorcycle just like his, the word "Faithful" scrawled across the engine. Kneeling on the seat is a classic-style pinup girl with big hazel eyes, messy blond hair half pulled up, a tattoo across her chest, and wearing hip-hugger jeans and a halter top.

She looks a lot like me.

Four

Tavish

I guess I thought this was going to be harder.

It's not that it's easy. Don't get me wrong, I'll be happy to go back to a world where my kit doesn't need to be ordered out on my bed and I can walk down the hall without swinging my arms like a douchebag. But I guess I was expecting that it'd be... more.

It's mostly just a mind game. You know one day to the next that even if you do something the exact same way two days in a row, chances are it'll be wrong one time and right the other. They want to know I can handle being yelled at and that I can handle orders even though I don't understand them. They want to be sure I'll conform.

What they don't know is that this is what I crave. This is why I'm here: being allowed to blend into a unit, having clear expectations in front of me and getting them done quietly. It makes me happy that if I do everything right, no one notices. They only notice if you screw up. Not being singled out or paid much attention is a great reward in my book.

My mom was always fussing over me like I was the only special snowflake in the pile. She pushed me to try art school even though it was clear that while I have some talent, I don't have *that* kind of talent—the kind that makes art into a career. Mom needed me to succeed. Even though I was still pretty young I can remember the blowout right before we moved out of my grandparents' place: "I can do this! Look at him, he's going to be something and then you'll see! I didn't need him, and I don't need you two, to raise a kid!" My success was my mom's success. It proved to the world that she was a good mom, and man, did she want to prove that. She just didn't want to work at it. Instead, she kept a revolving door of men in and out of the house and slept until mid-afternoon on the weekends, never helping with homework or reading me a book or even teaching me to cook before she expected me to make my own food—usually hers and her "friends" as well. I had to keep her secrets, too. That was the worst part. I guess it was a good thing I grew up bigger than most kids, because it didn't take me long to stop hiding in the closet and start sleeping with a baseball bat.

As shitty of a mother as she was, even though I could've run back to my grandparents', I couldn't leave her there, never knowing which one would finish her off. In the end, she met the one boyfriend who wasn't so keen on me living with them. She chose him over me, and back I went to my grandparents' house. I felt guilty for how relieved I was. It didn't stop her, though, from highlighting my every mediocre success as though it was her own. When I'd see her, she'd parade me in front of all our relatives and her friends. "Look at him, he joined a sports team! He got a decent report card! He got a job, got a driver's license, finished high school!"

I don't need someone to notice that I can do the things that are expected of everyone. Being rewarded by not being fussed over is excellent motivation.

We hit the halfway point or so of our training, which means a weekend away. Some guys go home, but my family is three provinces over from the recruit school here in Quebec, so I hitch a ride with some of the guys and head into Montreal. I'm sure as hell not sticking around here for the weekend.

The hotel we end up at is basically a shit-hole, but we're at a strip club within the hour. I'm sitting at a booth, picking at my dinner, trying to decide why anyone thought eating here was a good idea. Glancing around, I can't say as I'm confident in the health and safety record of this place. I consider heading back to the room and ordering food in, but none of the other idiots I came with can speak a word of French and I can; I have a feeling at least one of them might need to be bailed out by the end of the night, so I stick it out.

I feel like more of a grownup than most of these jokers, but at nineteen, I'm easily the youngest of this group, I'd say by a couple years or more. Some of these guys are married, and I think at least one even has a kid. Not that you can tell right now—they're almost all in pervert row, half in the bag already and hollering like rowdies. I'm guessing this happens a lot around here. Recruits on their weekend off aren't hard to miss with our shaved heads and dog tags indented under our shirts. I'm willing to bet more than a few guys will whip theirs out in the hope of impressing the ladies before the night is over, as though making it through a month of Basic Training gives them the right to claim some sort of hero soldier status.

It's not that I don't see the stripper. I'm still a guy, right? She's hot, I suppose, but a little bony for me and her tits are obviously fake. I'm sure she's wearing a wig, and I never understood the whole "clear plastic spike heels when you're naked" thing, but I guess that's why they're called stripper heels. She's not dancing, really, just prancing on the stage, twirling around the bar now and again, and bending over a lot. Still, the view's nice, if you can look past the heads of all the other guys watching her. When she looks up at me, though, all I see is Juliette.

I don't call back home much—I leave the phone for the guys with families and kids— but I'd called a buddy to check in a couple days ago, and last he heard she'd taken a job at some hole in the wall just like this. Not that I'm surprised, but that doesn't change the fact that I broke the handle of the pay phone I was using when I hung up. My head spins thinking about her up there, guys just like flicking loonies and begging a dance. It really isn't that big of a step away from the short shorts and halter top and bending over the beer tub. Both are selling sex, but every time I think of her for sale it rips me apart.

You can't help someone who doesn't want to be helped, right? I try to convince myself of that because every part of me feels personally responsible, like there was something I could've said or done that would've stopped her years ago, before she got this far. Not that this is the worst thing she could be doing, but I'm terrified of the next step for her. How long before she's selling more than a look? She's not on any stage because she feels empowered; she's there because she feels stuck. I know it. The truth is though that she didn't want me. She doesn't want me. God help me, I'd walk away from this, from the future I planned, if she asked me to come save her. Thing is, she never has and I doubt she ever will.

I see Silas out of the corner of my eye. Silas had been on the bus with me to the airport when we left for here. He's older than I am by a few years, we'd never met before but we've gotten along since then. It's easy to make friends in the military. We don't have to have much in common; we just get along because we're in it together. He's engaged, I saw his fiancé watching as the bus pulled away when we left Calgary. From here, it looks like the guys have roped him into a lap dance in the corner. There's a dancer in a G-string grinding on him, but his hands grip the sides of the chair. After a minute or so, he shoves some cash into the string on her side and gets up, walking over to sit with me.

"These guys are killing me," he mutters when he plops down on the bench across from me.

"You didn't seem to mind watching the show." I grin and he laughs back.

"Yeah, watching wasn't so bad. But you gotta have a line somewhere, you know?" He says that more to himself than to me as he watches the dancer move on to another lap. This recipient is far more accommodating to her charms.

It's around then things start spinning a little. I look down at the table and realize the disgusting sandwich is mostly uneaten, but I've got half a dozen beer bottles in front of me. Shit. I never drink this much, I'm still not a fan of losing control and I sure didn't intend to do it here. Silas is unconcerned with my food standards, he's always hungry. When he sees I'm not going to finish my meal, he pulls my plate over to himself and digs in. I grimace but he clearly doesn't care to see the health inspection on this place.

It feels like the music in the bar gets louder, but maybe I just stopped hearing everything else. It's playing Thin Lizzy's version of Whiskey in the Jar, which seems fitting though a strange choice for a place like this. I'm surprised it's not some top forty pop hit. I try to focus back on the stripper but my eye wanders to one of the waitresses. She's in a bikini top and those panties that are like tiny shorts and she's come over more than a few times tonight, even when I didn't need anything. She's short, with high heels, a smattering of tattoos and straight blond hair. It's probably dyed that colour but I don't really care. She nods at me and winks.

It's not like I waited for Juliette. I thought I might, once upon a time. The first time I met her I was just seventeen and still a virgin. Something about being the son of a single teen mom will do that to you. For the longest time I had this romantic notion to make her my first. It didn't take long for me to realize it was a lost cause. The worst is I don't think she remembers a lot of the times I picked her up. I doubt she realizes how many times she was the one to call because it was always when she was too far gone to know her own name. It used to make me unrealistically happy that she'd think of me, even in that place. I thought it meant that deep down she felt something, but maybe I was fooling myself and she just felt safe. I'm sure she just needed someone and knew I'd always come.

Six months or so after we met, she called once, using that sing song voice she did when she was trashed. It had only just warmed to spring then, weeks away from graduation, and by the time I got there, she was half asleep, leaned up against a play structure at a park by her place. Her parents thought she was sleeping at a friend's place so she didn't want to go home and answer their questions. She was wearing a tiny skirt so I handed her some wind pants from my bag and she stood inches from me when she just reached behind herself, unzipped and dropped her skirt, staring at my face the whole time, daring me to look while she very slowly pulled on the pants. I never dropped her eyes, even though it killed me to look at them dilated and vacant. I didn't have to look down to know she had nothing on underneath the skirt. She never did. I could smell him, whoever he was that night, on her and it took me longer than it should've to unclench my fists. I wanted to drag her back to wherever she'd come from and I wanted that asshole's blood on my hands. Instead, like I always did, I just led her to my bike and took her away from all of it.

That night we just drove, left the city and headed out to the foothills while the sun came up. She dozed a little behind me but she'd gotten good at linking her arms around me to keep herself steady. By the time I dropped her back at home that morning, I'd made up my mind. I went out with the team that night and took one of the cheerleaders up on her standing offer. We dated a few months, mostly just because I wasn't a one-night kind of guy. The relationship, such as it was, never felt right and I didn't feel bad when it ended. I actually felt relieved that she cared even less than I did.

It's funny, I took from some other girl exactly what I wouldn't take from Juliette.

After that, I realized I didn't have much of a stomach for the casual hook up; it became my habit that if I knew it was only going to be one night, I found other ways for us both to get off. It worked for me, and it was almost always just one night. It's hard to really date anyone when you're willing to drop everything to rescue another girl anytime she calls.

And I did, every time she asked. I'd tell myself I was just being a good friend, I was doing what anyone would, I was just looking out for her like a big brother. I might have fooled myself but I never fooled any other girl I was with when she'd call and I'd go. We'd drive around, in the summer sometimes stop at a park, when it was colder or later we'd grab a coffee. There had been so many nights I'd watched her sleep. Sitting in Denny's, I'd bring Juliette in drunk or high and I'd watch her come down. She'd sit on the bench with me, falling asleep on my shoulder. I remember one night one of the waitresses who had seen us so many times, she caught me twirling her hair in my fingers after she'd fallen asleep with her head in my lap. I was embarrassed at what they might think of me, so obviously pining over this girl. The waitress only said, "That girl doesn't know what a guy like you is worth."

I just sighed, "This girl doesn't know what *she's* worth." The waitress just gave me a sad smile, but after that, they stopped ever charging for our coffee.

I'd be lying to myself something fierce if I thought Juliette was back there waiting for me now. I know she thinks that it's all she has to offer, and a big part of her thrives on the control she feels by using it. No matter how much I try to remember the sound of her voice when she told me she didn't really have that choice anymore, I know I'm the only one hanging onto that part of her.

I think I've had too much to drink. I also think it's time to stop holding onto something that's not mine to protect.

I look at Silas as he's finishing up my sandwich, and then I look back over at the waitress. She's cashing out and she's kept her eyes my way. I know she's interested. I throw some money on the table and down the rest of my beer. I wait for Silas to say something about how this isn't like me, but he's just giving me an amused smirk. I realize he doesn't have the slightest clue if this is like me or not. None of them do, so I can be whoever I want. Right now, I want to be someone who's letting it go.

"No point in drawing a line without a reason to have one," I mutter, and half-stumble in her direction while she grins at me. The music is louder next to the speaker by the bar as I grab her hip and she follows me to one of the dark booths in the back, the ones with the curtain.

"m'uishe rinne me me don amada…"

***

It seems a little surreal, packing all this into barrack boxes to ship to the next location. This is really happening. I'm going to be an infantry soldier in the Canadian Forces.

I mean, I'm not a soldier yet. Not really. But I'm not a recruit anymore, either. Next week I start my trade training, and it won't be long into the new year when they'll assign me to a battalion. I'm hoping it'll be back out West, I tell myself it's to be close to Mom and make sure she's all right. Truth is if anything she's the only reason I'd rather stay East.

I finished my course as Top Candidate. I guess I didn't blend in as well as I thought, but Mom isn't coming for graduation so she doesn't need to know. Grandma and Gramps would be there if they could, they're far closer to what real parents would be anyways, but I told them it was okay, it's not a big deal. I know travel isn't easy for them and there's no sense in them coming all this way when I could only really spend one evening with them. Gramps was a soldier, too, in the artillery. He served during the Korean War and he's the real reason I'm here in the first place. I know they all think I'm chasing some ghost of the dad I never met, but truth be told, as much as I think I'm supposed to feel some sort of need to find my "real" father, I never have. Gramps, he's never treated me as any less than his own son, even when he was stuck with the responsibility of me after he should've been done raising kids. I can only hope to be the man he is one day. He's the only one I told about the award, I mentioned it when I called over the weekend. He said, "It's easy to be the best of the idiots."

Man, I love him.

We're all basically in a hold pattern while our course wraps up and we wait for the graduation parade this week, so it's not surprising that we are still in the small social area just before nine a.m. All of us are just nervous energy, wasting time before we stand at attention one last time in this place and finally walk out for good. Silas and I play cards. I think we both forgot to bet on the last several hands, we're too lazy even for that. None of us pay much attention to what's on the screens until someone suddenly jumps up to flip on the volume. That's when we watch a plane crash into some building in New York City. There's confusion and a little chaos in the room as we all try to understand the equally confused and terrified commentators but by the end of the morning, it looks like one thing is clear.

Holy shit.

I'm going to war.

Five

2006

Juliette

I don't know what possessed me to send in the application or write the essay for admittance, but standing here after work at the mailbox of my apartment building at one a.m., I look at an envelope from the college. No matter what the letter inside says, it's a big fucking deal. One I have no idea if I'm ready for.

I can't keep moving from apartment to apartment, and at twenty-four, I'm getting too old to be prancing around, selling the idea of sex for a living. Even I know there's no job security in that, and it's getting tiring keeping up the look I need to do it. Truth is, I'm not really too old. Not yet. I'd just rather get out of this before I'm one of those girls who *is* too old and doesn't know it. Who am I kidding, anyway? I might still be young, but I'm tired of all this. I want to try while I still have something in me that thinks I can.

I'm already in my third apartment since I moved out from my parents' place five years ago. Roommates come and go, and so have the jobs. After a year of taking it all off, I've tried to stick to the clubs where I can at least keep a little on while I wait tables or hand out beers. It's depressing that I've never even bothered learning to be a bartender. That might actually feel like a real career, but instead I've stuck to jobs where the main requirements are that the drunks can see my hip bones and I'm up for anything. It's like a comfort blanket. At least I know I'm good at that. Can't fail if I don't try, right? That sounds a lot like someone can't steal what I give away. Both seem to apply to every job I've ever had.

Also, every guy I've ever had, if I think about it.

Not that I've had too many of those. I mean, I date a lot. I still call it dating, because part of me still pretends there's romance involved. It hides the fact that I was still in high school when I stopped counting how many guys I'd slept with, and it puts a pretty bow on the fact that my dates usually just last the night. Sometimes the hour. Rarely more than a week.

Then there's my attempt at relationships. I think at first I was trying to replace him, but eventually I gave up. No matter how long I let them in or what I offered, no one ever looked at me like that again. Why would they? Who wants to be on call to pick up a pathetic mess at all hours, or sit in silence all night and stare at the sky? Some of these guys might be willing to listen to me giggle on the phone for a bit while I come down, but none of them have the patience to talk me down when I'm sure my skin is melting off, or the numbers on my clock are coming to get me. I cut out the hard stuff a couple years ago, when someone at a party I was at just didn't wake up, but I can't pretend that just because I'm not using means I have my shit together. Besides, only one person has ever preferred me sober.

Right now, there's someone sharing my bed. Scott works as a bouncer at the same club I work at. I'm not stupid, I know he just likes the *idea* of me: a girlfriend who works at the club, who's easy to show off to his friends. His job is to keep the peace and the employees safe, but I swear he likes watching me get grabbed all night. It reinforces his sense of pride in getting to take me home, knowing others were interested. It feels nice sometimes, the way I can make him feel special just by looking good enough in a low-cut shirt. I don't think it'd take too much thinking, though, to realize that's not a long-term relationship in the making. I can't make forever out of being someone's trophy.

Scott had caught me at a weak moment. If I'm not hopping bed to bed, I'm never alone. I'm usually someone's girl. Whether it's for an hour, a night, a week or a few months, life is easy this way. It's a powerful feeling. I never mind where my guys have been or what they've been doing. Or who. I convinced myself that it's romantic because I'm the one they crawl back to, or that I'm something special because they come to me eventually. The truth is harder to forgive myself for—that I let them come to me as their last resort on the nights they're desperate for comfort or release. The rare time that they want to make it last, I usually let them. I'd even be exclusive if they asked, whether they were or not. I always like it when they claim me and let others know I'm theirs. I'm no one, so it's nice every once in a while to be someone, even if it's just the someone that someone else was sleeping with. It never takes long before they move on and leave me to do the same.

I know it's never real, and it certainly isn't with Scott. Hell, if I thought it was, I'd have told him about the college application before now. I didn't though. I just downed a couple beers and filled out the application one night while he was working. I meant it, though, because the next day I requested transcripts and completed the essay, mailing it in as quickly as I could with the registration fee, paid with a money order I bought with that night's tips, before I could change my mind.

It has been hard, running into so many of my acquaintances from school these past few years and realizing how many of them are finishing university and starting real lives. I just want a chance to do that, even a few years late. So, I guess this letter will make or break that. Either I give up and just let this life happen, or I head a few hours north and see if I can be one of those people who has a real career—a real future.

I'm terrified that I'm not cut out to ever be one of those people.

I'm still staring at the unopened letter when my phone rings. My cell phone is my biggest luxury. When I moved out, I kept the phone and the number and hung on, paying the bill myself even when it took more of my pay than the utilities. It makes me feel like I have a connection to the world, a constant, a little piece of control. I grab it from my purse and stare. It's from an unknown number. I don't recognize the area code. I consider ignoring it, but it's the middle of the night, so I'm worried something's wrong. I answer and it's quiet for a moment. Then I hear, "Hey."

I'm amazed I still know that voice.

"Hey, Slick." My voice is low, like I'm worried I might scare him off. I haven't heard from him in years. After he left for Basic Training, I thought maybe he'd get in touch, maybe he'd call one day when he was done, but he never did.

I'd thought of him, though. When those planes hit the Twin Towers, it was all I thought about that day. I tried to imagine the quiet kid on the black Ninja going to war, but I couldn't. I saw the news like everyone else when the soldiers left soon after. My head tried to convince me he wouldn't have been done training in time to leave that quickly, but I still scanned every clip for his among all those dusty faces. I never saw him and as the years passed, his memory faded in my mind to more of a warmth, a happy place I'd let myself drift off to when I was walking or on the train headed home.

"Can I give you a ride home?" he asks. I laugh.

"Actually, I'm already home. Where are you?" I realize I don't even know where in the country he lives.

"I'm at my grandparents', visiting. Are you... I mean, can I..."

"Meet me at the Victoria train station," I say. "I can be there in ten."

This is probably not a good idea.

SIX

Tavish

This is probably not a good idea.

It's funny what knowing you're going to war will inspire you to do. By the time I got to the battalion after training, I was too late to go to Afghanistan with the rest of the boys the first time. Instead, it wasn't too long before they sent me on some sun-tanning deployment as a peacekeeper. It almost killed me, standing on useless checkpoints like a lazy asshole while there were soldiers in a fucking war. But I can only go where I'm told, so that's where I went.

My number has finally been called, though. I'm headed to Kandahar in a couple of weeks, which is exactly what I trained to do. What I want to do. I've spent five years on peacekeeping deployments, domestic deployments for natural disasters, military competitions, training—so much training. We are always training. It feels like it's been five years of everything but. Everything but war.

Everything but her.

I've filled my time home with distractions. After Montreal, I realized I still wasn't a one-night kind of guy, but I've gotten even better at all the other ways I could enjoy my time without taking it all. I've found more than a few back booths and back seats in the past five years.

I'm not a saint; I just save sex for the sad excuses that I call relationships these days. Even those don't last long and seem few and far between. Turns out the world isn't crawling with women who want to spend their time waiting for a guy to come home. Fair enough. The Canadian Forces isn't exactly the most glamorous or highest paying gig out there, and once the lure of the uniform wears off, you're left with a bunch of missed birthdays and last minute goodbyes.

I have a few weeks of pre-deployment leave, and at the last minute, I decide I'm not going to spend it in my apartment with my roommate Jason and his girlfriend, listening to them "say goodbye." I don't need a reminder that no one will be waiting for me when I leave. It's easier that way. So, I drive down here with Silas to visit my grandparents while he spends time with his fiancée Beth's family and his mom. I know if I'm here I should see my mom, too, but I've even been putting that off.

It takes a couple of days here before I come clean with myself: I've been hoping to see *her*, too. Another day to admit there is a reason I've always transferred her number into every new phone I got.

I don't want to die without seeing her again.

I'm so melodramatic; up until this year, it has been a quiet war for Canada, considering, but things are getting messy. Last month, I filled out paperwork on who would carry my body home and receive my Memorial Cross. This isn't another training exercise and being forced to make those kinds of plans when you're twenty-four puts a lot of things into perspective. It's what's pushing me to make this call.

When I dial her, I've convinced myself there is no way she has the same number. Even if she does, what kind of jerk calls someone he hasn't spoken to in five years at one a.m.? This kind, I guess. That's how we seemed to work, though—phone calls long past when regular people should make them. Night-time rides and midnight coffee. We'd never been out together to do anything normal. I'm just hoping after all this time she remembers, and, well, at least she's willing to see me.

As I pull up to the mostly vacant train station to meet her, I see the glow of her cigarette as she sits on the steps. I realize looking at her I should never have agreed to have her meet me here. With her elbows on her knees, that shirt is doing nothing to hide anything. She has a lot more ink. The tattoo on her chest now spreads across her shoulder and completely down one arm. It's almost one thirty at night downtown and this place is almost entirely deserted, but she's still just sitting there, oblivious to what might happen. She has never had much in the way of situational awareness. I think I might have too much.

My bike announces my presence long before I arrive, and she stands when she sees me and walks down the steps. I can see the logo of one of the local nightclubs stretched across the front of her shirt; she was probably awake when I called because she was working there. I don't know if I'm more disappointed that she's still doing that kind of work, or happy that place isn't a strip club.

She cocks her head when she comes over and grins.

"That's no crotch rocket there, Slick."

It sure isn't. When I returned from Bosnia, I traded in the Ninja for a Fat Boy with the money from my deployment. The beat-up truck that sits in the garage all summer is a reminder that I probably could've made a smarter investment, but that old bike was just the best I could afford when I was in my teens. I've always wanted a Harley and I spent six months in some crappy country, bored out of my skull, to earn her.

"Nope, she's a fair deal better than that. And has a seat, too, so hop on."

Juliette unbuckles the helmet I'd strapped to the back. I told myself when I bought the bike that having the backrest was just practical, but as much as I loved having her pressed against me on all our long rides years ago, I knew it had been terribly uncomfortable for her. Deep down, I bought this bike with her on my mind.

When she pulls herself up on the back, she stops for a minute, then leans back.

"Wow, isn't this luxurious! I have so much room!" She moves her hips back and forth on the seat, I think to demonstrate how much space is there, but my brain stops processing thought at that point. Her hands touch my sides briefly, but then she pulls them back. I realize that she doesn't know if she's still supposed to hold on to me with that seat there. Technically, she doesn't have to, but this isn't going to work for me.

"Put your hands back or I'll take that backrest right off," I growl. Something about this girl makes me crazy, and I'm already acting like a possessive jerk again. She laughs and I close my eyes for a second at the sound. It's been a long five years fooling myself. I could listen to her laugh all night. When she slides her hands around my middle and presses against my back, I didn't know it was possible to miss something that much without realizing it until you get it back.

I drive around for a while, looping through downtown and into some old neighbourhoods, just enjoying the feel of her pressed against me, before stopping at a mostly rundown children's park. Juliette hops off and by the time I've parked the bike and taken off my helmet, she's on one of the swings, grinning over at me.

"So, stranger, want to tell me where you've been hiding?" She's pumping her legs in and out to swing higher, her hair almost covering her face with each swing back. I head over and sit on the swing next to her, but I'm so distracted by her back and forth that I never really start moving.

"Well, when I finished my training I was posted up to Edmonton. And basically, that's where I've been for five years. I went overseas once—" she suddenly puts her feet down, kicking up the sand underneath as she skids to a stop, and stares over at me, "—just to Bosnia. I was too late to get to go to Afghanistan back then. It's been just exercises and training this past bit, though I did get to tour British Columbia a while back. Would have been pretty if it hadn't been on fire."

Juliette smiles faintly at my joke but she's still staring at me with an odd look on her face. "What? Not what you were expecting in a soldier?" I laugh.

"I watched the news for months," she mutters under her breath.

"What?"

She's louder now, angry, looking anywhere but at me. "After 9/11. I watched the news every day for months! I studied every clip that showed faces when they sent soldiers to Afghanistan. I had no idea where you were or if you went." She looks back at my face. "I was scared. I was worried that maybe, if something happened to you, you know, maybe I'd never know. Then, when soldiers were killed and I'd see it on the news, I was terrified one day that's how I'd learn I'd never get to see you again."

I'm off my swing before she finishes the sentence and I pull her up and wrap her in my arms. "Jules, I had no idea. I didn't even think, I just didn't want you to think you had to keep in touch, you know. When I first started training, I didn't know where in the country I'd end up, and once I got to Edmonton, I didn't want to bug you, especially when keeping in touch with me sucks because I'm never home. I thought you'd rather I didn't make you feel like you had to try to keep track of me."

"I'm a big girl," she mutters into my chest. "I can decide if I want the chance to stay friends with someone. And I wanted to stay friends with you." My back stiffens at the word friends, but I know what I promised, even if it was seven years ago, I promised friends and then I cut her off just because I was worried I couldn't keep it in my pants. Now I'm making her see me again at the exact time I have nothing to offer her. I'm an asshole.

"I'm sorry, Jules. I'm so sorry. I was a terrible friend, and I'm afraid I'm about to be an even worse one."

She pulls back from me a little and looks up at me, her eyes peeking from under my chin. I think one of my favourite parts of seeing her so late is that whatever makeup she used to hide herself in the day is virtually gone by now. Faint dark hues around her lashes are the only hint of any colour. She's gorgeous this way, when her face shows through her mask.

"I'm leaving for Afghanistan next week."

Her mouth drops open a little bit and she stares at me. I can tell she's processing what I said to try to think of the right response. Eventually, she shakes her head slightly and steps away.

"You always seem to have something to say that I don't know how to respond to," she says.

"You don't have to say anything, Juliette. It is what it is. I came back here to see my family for a bit before I leave and I just couldn't help myself when I was here. I wanted to see you. I hope that's okay."

We are silent for a minute, then she takes my coat and throws it on the ground, lying down on top of it. I lie down next to her and we stare at the sky, even though there are only a handful of stars visible through the clouds.

"Always," she whispers. "It's always okay." Then she lays her head on my chest and I hear her breathing relax. After a minute, she starts asking questions and we talk about where life has brought us. If I close my eyes, we could be seventeen again and I feel more content than I have in five years. Suddenly, she sits up and rummages through her purse, pulling out a folded envelope and staring at it awhile.

"So... I applied to Grant McEwan college," she says. "Totally not a big deal, I mean, it's just college and a two-year program and with my crappy grades I probably won't get in, even to that... Can you see me in college? I wouldn't last... I didn't even do my homework in high school. It's silly, really..." She starts stuffing the envelope back in her purse, and I snatch it from her hands.

"Stop that." I'm probably a little more forceful than I need to be, but I've never heard Juliette ever consider something like this and I wasn't going to let her dismiss it. "That's amazing! What did you apply for?"

"Media and Communication Studies. I could eventually transfer to an undergrad if I wanted when I'm done but for now even with the grants and stuff... I mean, even if I do get in... I really haven't thought this through." I tilt her chin up to look at me so she'll stop.

"Hey. Hey, you know what? This is amazing and I'm already proud of you just for applying. Why haven't you opened that yet?" She just stares at the letter for a minute.

"Because if I didn't get in, I figure it's just a sign that this," she gestures to herself, "is me, and I'll just have to keep finding jobs like this until I can't, and then find the jobs people like this do after we can't do those jobs anymore, and that will be me. I don't know if I'm ready to accept that. But if I did get in, I'll need to try. Now that I think about it, I think that's scarier. I'm not a trier. I'm a quitter. I half-ass things and I put off things and I fail at things. I don't try. Nobody would believe I'd make it anyways... I didn't even tell Scott I applied. That way he can't make fun of me when I don't get accepted." There's something behind her eyes when she says this. She mentioned the guy when we were catching up, and if I didn't already irrationally despise him just for sleeping in her bed, I hate him even more now.

"Open it."

Juliette looks at it a minute longer, then rips it open and glances over the cover letter, just staring at it, and her eyes shine. I'm not sure what the right answer is here. I hear her breath hitch.

"Jules, no matter what—"

"I'm accepted," she whispers.

I grab her into a hug so fast I crush the paper between us. She's laughing now but there's tears in her eyes, too. This is huge for her. This is change and growing up and this is *trying*. Something real. I feel like this could be it for her; this could make the difference.

"I have no idea what I'll do now," she whispers into my shirt while she laughs.

"You're going to have to tell what's his name," I grumble, trying to pretend like I don't remember exactly what his name is, along with a hundred ways I could kill him with my bare hands. All that training has got to be good for something.

"I guess. He's... I mean... Fuck it, Slick, I never meant for him to come with me on this. We're not... I mean, this will mean him and I are done. Which is sad, now that I think of it. We should've been done a long time ago if I'm this ready to let him go. Probably could've skipped all of it, really. We're just messing around. So, the only part that will matter to him will be the part where he'll need to find a new apartment or take my lease... I need to move out to Edmonton. I guess I have to take a couple trips and look for a job and a place to stay and a roommate... I don't have much time to get all that done before classes start."

"Hey!" Suddenly, I have the best idea. "My apartment will have a room when I'm gone! My roommate's girlfriend is going to stay in his room, but my room is going to be sitting empty. You can stay there, you know, until you figure out where you want to be, just cover what you can and take time to see the area. It's not far from the college and you'd have six months at least before I'm back." All I can think is that this plan means she moves away from this Scott asshole that much sooner. I'm trying not to also admit that it also means I'm connecting her to me, just a little, while I'm gone.

Juliette looks at me like I have two heads. "You know I wouldn't be able to afford whatever apartment you're in. What if your roommate's girlfriend hates me? You trust me with all your stuff? I don't know what to say—"

"Jules, think about it. My place was just going to be sitting there this whole time, so you just pay me whatever you're paying where you are now. Either way, it's more than I'd have with no one there. You can do this! Move in there and take your time to find a job and funding. You can start paying rent once you've got that squared away. Besides, I didn't trust Marissa to feed Gunner anyways."

"Uh... What's a Gunner? And who's Marissa?"

"Gunner is my fish. He's very high maintenance, because every time I accidentally kill him, it costs me ten dollars at the pet store to buy another Gunner." She grins. "Marissa is my roommate Jason's girlfriend. He's on the same rotation as me, so he's leaving soon too and she's staying, so she'll be there."

"I... I need to think this all out, Slick. I really hadn't thought I'd be accepted. I have no real plan here. All I did was check to see if I could afford it, and I know I can get a few grants. I already applied for them, but I never really considered the rest of it..."

"Think it over tonight, okay? Just think. I have brunch with my family in the morning, but I'll give you a call after that and we can talk it out, okay?"

As I drop her off at her building hours later, I realize I have no idea what all this means, but I feel like I just threw Juliette an anchor.

Seven

Juliette

I know he's with his mom and grandparents, but I find myself pressing his contact on my phone anyway. My hands are shaking. My whole everything is shaking. I knew this wasn't who I was.

I've never told Tavish much about Scott. Why would he want to know? I haven't told him that the man has a temper like a wild animal. One minute he's fine, the next the table is in the hallway and dinner is all over the floor. When he flew off the handle at work with the unruly guests, it used to impress me. Here is a big strong guy, dominating, being protective of the club, of us. But it doesn't take long to realize that isn't it, really. He isn't fighting because he wants to protect something; he fights because he loses control. And he always loses control.

I want to say he's the first violent guy I've dated, but that would be a lie. There have been more than a few, but I've usually known quickly and never ended up too hurt before I break things off. I also want to say Scott has never raised a hand to me and that's why I let him stay around, but that would be a lie, too. He raises his hand to me a lot, but he's never followed through. It is always just there, the threat that ends the argument, the same gesture that both terrifies me in the moment and stands as some kind of proof of his good-guy status when it's all over. "Stop being so dramatic," he'd say. "I've never laid a hand on you. Even when you make me lose my temper, I've always controlled myself." And that is true. But that control looks more and more like a threat every time his hand hovers there, right above my face.

I know deep down this is probably why I never told him about the application. Me doing something that makes me more than what I am, the idea that I might move on and he'd still be there, I knew that would push him. I also have never intended to include him in the plan. I've assumed he knows this has never been that kind of relationship. It's not forever, it's just for now. This morning I needed to pull off this band-aid and just make a concrete commitment to it before I convince myself to hide the letter and pretend none of it happened.

When I get home near dawn he's fast asleep. I realize he'd never even called to see where I was when I didn't come home. He doesn't really care. It's barely still morning before we crawl out of bed, which is standard for us since we both work late nights. When I make the coffee, I finally just blurt it out, still looking at the machine and not at him across the table.

"Scott, I'm leaving to move up to Edmonton. I'm sorry, but I got accepted to college up there and I'm going to try it out. I've had a lot of fun with you, but we knew this wasn't going to last forever. I'm going to move out at the end of the month. If you want, I could have them switch the apartment over to you." I get it all out quick. I don't want him to have the chance to lose his temper and not hear what I'm saying.

"What? Where the hell is this coming from? What the fuck, Juliette? You can't just spring that... College? You don't go to college. You're a fucking tub girl. Are you going to learn how to wiggle your ass better, or how to show your tits more? THAT'S what you do, Juliette. You're not going anywhere."

He looks back down at his coffee like that's the end of the conversation. He's not even raising his voice yet, like it's all a joke. Maybe he's hoping it is. His words slice through me but I try to ignore them. "I'm serious, Scott. I'm leaving and I'm going to college. You knew. I mean, this was never forever. You'll find someone else." I can see his fists clenching, and I know he's going to lose control. I'd planned for this, lying in bed when I couldn't sleep. I go to grab my purse.

"I'm going to Starbucks and grab a breakfast sandwich or something and give you some time. But I'm moving, Scott. I'm going to college and shit like that, what you just said to me? That's why we weren't going to work out."

He grabs my arm as I reach for my purse and holds on. He raises his other hand to my face like he always does, so I'm not prepared when this time it smashes into my jaw. I can taste blood in my mouth. I look up at him, expecting him to immediately react with horror at what he's done, apologize, anything. Instead, I just see rage and, I'm sure, disgust.

"You're not going anywhere, not right now, not later and not to Edmonton. Definitely not college. Do you understand? You're a FUCKING TUB GIRL, JULIETTE, and you're staying here with me until I say so."

I can feel my pulse pounding in my chest and hear it in my ears. I snatch my arm away, grab my bag and bolt to the door, then race down the steps. I don't think he's following me since he was only in his boxer shorts, but at this point I almost believe he would. I don't stop until I hit the coffee shop down the street, and that's when I pull out the phone.

I don't even know if he'll answer, but he does after just the first ring. "Hey! I'm just leaving the restaurant—"

"Slick..." I realize I have no idea what I'm going to say.

"Jules? What's wrong?"

"I told Scott today. I don't think I can go back to my apartment right now... I think I maybe need to get away from this coffee shop, too, he knows I'm here... I don't... I don't know what to do, Tavish." I know my voice is cracking and I must sound like a complete loser right now. Why did I call him? I haven't seen him in five years, and after one night out, I'm dumping this completely messed up life right on his lap. This might not be all that unbelievable for my life, but I'm sure his life looks a lot less ridiculous.

"Juliette, where are you? Are you okay? Did he hurt you?" I can hear whispers in the background and I don't even know how to answer. I'm in the middle of the coffee shop and people are already looking. I don't want them to hear me say anything. I tell him where I am.

"I'll be there as soon as I can, but if you see him, you stay around as many people as possible and you call me, okay?"

Less than half an hour later, I'm regretting the Americano because now I'm even shakier. Tavish walks in with someone else. From our conversation last night, I'm assuming it's his Army buddy that is visiting down here, too. He scans the shop then his eyes fix on me. I stand and I can see the exact moment they see my lip, which stopped bleeding but is puffed out, and my jaw, which is still a little red with the faint outline of what clearly looks like a hand. His entire face changes and it takes him just a few strides before he's standing right in front of me.

"Did he do this?" His voice is restrained, but as he runs his thumb along my bottom lip and cups my jaw in his hand, his whole body is shaking. I immediately step back. His friend puts a hand on his chest.

"Hey, man. You're scaring her. We'll sort this out, but you need to relax."

Tavish closes his eyes for a minute and takes a deep breath. Then he looks back at me and puts out his arms slowly, inviting me in. I bury myself in his chest, and all I hear is his heartbeat and his whispers reminding me to breathe. I don't even notice that we are moving until we end up sitting in the back of a truck parked on the road.

"Jules, I need you to tell me what happened. Has he done this before? Tell me you haven't been living like this? Please..."

I take a deep breath. "No! I mean, he threatens to all the time, but he's never actually hit me before. Telling him I'm leaving just sent him over the edge, I guess. I'm sure he's more upset about losing the apartment than about losing me—it's okay, really. I'm grateful that you came, but I just needed to get away for the day until he goes to work, then I'll figure it out. I had kind of hoped to get some of my things from there, just in case he loses it and runs off with my stuff, but I hadn't planned for it to go this bad. Really, it's okay."

"No!" I can see Tavish fighting to stay calm in front of me, but it's not the same as it is with Scott. It feels safe with him. "Do you know how many times I just picked you up and let some asshole get away with whatever he'd done with you? I was way too much of a pushover in high school, but I'm not a teenager anymore, Jules, and I'm not scared of this guy. We're going back to your apartment right now and you're going to get whatever you need while Silas and I inform him that he needs to find a new place to live."

I look over to his friend in the front seat. I realize I haven't even acknowledged him yet. He's cute, a little more baby faced than Tavish though he seems older, with light blond hair in that same short cut and almost pastel blue eyes. He's got one hand on the wheel and one on the armrest as he's turning, looking at us. He's a little smaller than Tavish, but I can tell he's all lean muscle under a loose-fit collared t-shirt that exposes a mosaic of colourful tattoos. After all Tavish's intensity, there's more of a relaxed feel from him, and even before he speaks, I can tell their personalities are very different. I wish I could've met him virtually any other way. This can't be a good first impression.

"Hey." He nods. "My name's Silas. And he's right, we'll sort this mess, just tell me where you live and we'll go there now. We're not easily intimidated." He smirks a little at that, and I just stare at him and let it all sink in. I don't understand what they think they're going to do, but I just nod. It will be nice to not have to find a couch to crash on until I find somewhere else. I'd figured Scott was going to be mad, but I also kind of thought he'd just accept it eventually, maybe stay at his friend's place or even on our couch until I left. I was planning to move, I know, but not *tonight*.

My heart is pounding as we walk up the stairs to the apartment. Part of me is just desperately hoping he's not there, but the rest knows that I need him to be there so this can be over. When we get to my door, I try to get my key from my purse but my hands are shaking. Tavish puts his hand on mine until I relax and then squeezes me from the side with his arm before we go in.

"Done having your little hissy—" Scott has put jeans on but not a shirt, and he stands up from the couch when he hears me walk in. His words die on his lips as he sees Tavish and Silas, who immediately stand in front of me. He looks back and forth from them to me a few times, completely confused. I don't have a lot of people I'd consider good friends, and he's never met any guys that he'd think might come to my rescue.

Come to my rescue... Is that what they've done? I look up at them both and realize I'd be devastated if they were to get hurt dealing with this garbage just for me. Tavish is a big guy, he always has been, well over six feet and strong. Silas is only slightly smaller, but the way they carry themselves is more intimidating than their size. They are both standing there, shoulders back, one foot slightly forward. Tavish is opening and closing his fists at his side. When he was younger, it used to come off more as a nervous tic, but now it looks menacing. Silas is just absently tapping the middle finger on his right hand against his thigh. I think Silas might even be smirking. They look the opposite of intimidated by Scott, who at this point walks towards us. He's maybe a bit taller than Tavish and wider. He's got a lot of muscle from time at the gym and what I've always guessed were a few extra "supplements" on the side, but he's also soft from too much drinking, late nights and crappy food. One thing is for sure; watching him approach us, he looks a whole lot less sure of himself than they do.

"What the hell, bitch? You had to bring some random guys into our business?" He's getting a little closer, but he still hasn't come right up to us. I think he might be scared, which is funny because he's a bouncer. He's thrown out all kinds of guys from the club. I guess it's a different story when he's completely on his own. I open my mouth to say something, but Tavish speaks up.

"You don't have any 'business' anymore, asshole. She's here to get some of her things and then you're going to take the day to find another place to live. You will not be here when she gets back tonight. Do you understand?" His voice is angry but controlled, and he punctuates every word like a command. Silas turns to look at me and nods towards the hallway. He follows me as I walk towards the bedroom. Tavish doesn't even blink; his eyes are fixed on Scott.

"Should you, I mean, should we leave him there by himself?" I whisper at Silas as we walk down the hall.

"What?" Silas looks at me, almost confused, then grins. "Oh! Don't you worry, Love. Tav will be just fine. Thing about Tavish is, he doesn't start many fights." Now I'm more nervous, but Silas quietly laughs and tugs me into my room. "He's really good at finishing them, though." He winks at me. I don't really know how to take that, but Silas doesn't seem in the least bit concerned about leaving Tavish out there with Scott, so I'll have to trust him.

I don't have a lot of things to pack. I pull an old duffel bag from the closet and throw my clothes and shoes in it. I grab my old hand-me-down laptop from my sister, the shoebox from the closet, my little stuffed Grover. As I move to the bathroom, I see Silas pull something from the wall, and he hands me my phone charger. I'd have completely forgotten. I run into the bathroom for my toiletries and makeup, realizing when I see it that I'm not wearing any. Crap, I'm a hot mess. I avoid looking in the mirror. I just want to get anything I don't want him to take out of spite while I'm gone, and he would, so I sweep my cosmetics and hair products off the counter and into the bag, and head back out to the hall.

Back in the kitchen where we came in, Tavish and Scott haven't moved. I let him know I have what I want, and he tells Scott one more time that he needs to be out by tonight. I'm almost relaxing at how uneventful it all was when I open the door and Scott spits at us.

"I don't know who you are, but I'm guessing you don't know her. She's just some bar whore, you know. She'll give up on college when she realizes her tits won't guarantee she passes. I give it a month before you realize she wasn't worth it."

I don't even get all the way turned around before I hear Tavish's fist connect with Scott's nose. By the time I can see them both, Tavish's hands are back up and Scott is down on the floor, blood oozing from the hand over his face. He's only down for a moment, but when he jumps up to lunge forward, Silas is the one to shove him.

"Listen, you piece of shit, there's not much I hate more than a guy who thinks hitting a woman makes him a big man, and I'd love to watch my boy here lay you out, but you're not worth our time. Think about it. This won't end well for you, and if you try that here again, not only will you not get back up next time, but she'll call the cops with that split lip and send you to lockup. Pack your shit and get out. We don't want to see you again."

I feel Silas push me gently out the door. Tavish doesn't turn his back on Scott until it clicks behind us.

I was right. This is what it feels like to be rescued.

Eight

Tavish

I'm willing to bet this isn't the first time some asshole has put his hands on her, but this is the first time I've manned up enough that I'm not going to walk away and let it go. There's still that voice in my head, though, that reminds me I have no right and I have no idea what I'm doing. I haven't seen her in five years and the next day I'm throwing her douchebag boyfriend out? I need to get a grip.

I get in the backseat of the truck with her again, leaving Silas in the front like a rough-looking cab driver. He looks back to me and I nod, so he pulls his truck out onto the road and starts to head back to my grandparent's house. Two things the Army has taught me are that when it's negative thirty and you're in a tent, you spoon, and once you've spooned with someone enough times, you can talk without words. Sometimes, I think he can read my mind. I know a lot of times I can read his. There are times when it's a pain in the ass, but it can come in handy in situations like this. He drops us off and heads back to where he's staying with Beth. He doesn't need me to thank him. He already knows.

I throw Juliette's bag in the front door, and I plop down next to her on the front step where she's lighting a cigarette with shaky hands. The adrenalin of the morning is wearing off, and I can see the tell-tale signs that she's going to crack. I've seen it in soldiers before; no one can feel invincible forever. It will eventually catch up with you. I don't think I've ever seen her cry. It's one of those things about herself she doesn't give away. For a girl who would hand herself over so easily to be used, she has still guarded tiny parts that she holds onto out of pride. She puts her hands over her face and takes a few deep breaths. When she puts them down, her eyes are red but dry. She's strong, but I'm worried it's eventually going to catch up with her and I'm even more concerned she'll be alone when it happens. Time and age haven't changed this ingrained need to protect her—if anything, they've made it more resolved. I resist the urge to hold her. I don't want to push things with her when she's so vulnerable. Then again, I feel like I've spent years not wanting to push her. Maybe it's time I should.

She's almost done with her smoke before she speaks, her lighter clicking back and forth in her hand. "I have no idea what I'm going to do. I can't go to work, he'll be there! Yesterday I wasn't even totally sure I wanted to move and try school, and now it looks like that's my only choice. I'm not ready, Tavish. I don't have a job there either. I can't find a place to live with no job..."

I put my arm around her gently. She's shaking, so I jump up and run inside, coming out thirty seconds later with one of my grandmother's quilts to wrap around us both. "Follow me up to my apartment when I head back." I surprise myself with that, but when I realize what I said, the plan seems to make perfect sense in my head. "My apartment is furnished already. You can stay there and look for a job. I told you, I'm not that worried about rent. You can give me something once you find work." I only add that part because she's not going to agree to live there for free. I'm going to have to pay the rent anyways, so it doesn't matter if someone stays there. I swallow the part of me that's unreasonably pleased to have the chance to keep her at my place when I'm gone.

Juliette stares at me like I have three heads. "I can't... I mean, I'm not ready—"

"Why? What do you need to do? Is there something else here for you?" That might have been the wrong thing to say.

"You really don't think much of me, do you? I have friends, you know, and this wasn't a bad job! I know I don't really talk to my parents, but they're here too..." I know she's mad, but I'm not done pushing yet.

"Jules, I don't mean it like that. I know starting somewhere new is hard, but you were already going to have to do that if you started school. This is just forcing your hand to make that step. It's only three hours away, just a bus trip and I know you have a license so you can borrow my truck if you need. You can come back and see family. You want this, and now you can do it."

Her face almost looks hopeful before it crumbles. She stares at her smoke as it slowly burns towards her fingers. "He wasn't wrong, you know," she almost whispers.

"Who wasn't, Jules?"

"Scott. He's not wrong. I'm just a bar whore. I was working at strip clubs while you were gone, did you know that? I bet you don't want to help me now, do you? I'm not even a good stripper. I've always been a little too short, too jiggly, too soft. How pathetic that I even fail at that? There's ways to make working at a bar a real job, a career even. People do it, but I'm not that person. I've never tried. I just bounce from bar to bar with no skill really except bending over to grab a drink. I'm not some college girl, the kind who do this job for a while before they move on to something better... I've been a bar slut since before I was even supposed to be in a bar. This is a bad idea, I don't—"

I've heard enough. I snatch the cigarette from her hand and toss it on the cement before I scoop her up onto my lap. She's still shaking and it's not the cold. I hold her for a moment longer than I should've, my face in her hair, breathing her in.

"Breathe, Jules."

I feel her match her breath to mine until her body slows. I stand up and set her back on the step in front of me. Stepping back, I crouch a little so I'm at eye level with her.

"What you've done isn't who you are. I knew you were stripping, and it only bothered me because I hate that other guys leered at you like that. It doesn't change my opinion of you. Whether you're a stripper, a waitress or a college student, I'm here. I learned seven years ago, I can't make you do anything, no matter how much I wish I could. But if you want to do this, I'll do whatever I can to help you see it through. You're beautiful, you're smart, you're independent and you absolutely can be something new if you want to."

Juliette stares at me for a long moment, then plops back down on the step and lights another cigarette. I almost open my mouth to say something about how she's going to kill herself but decide against pushing my luck. She's had a rough morning. After a few minutes, she looks up at me with tired eyes.

"Okay." It sounds almost like a sigh, but I'll take it.

"I'll go back tonight and take what he's left, I guess. I got most of it for free anyways, so I'll just put the rest on the curb for other people to take. Then I'll go with you. My lease was only month to month. It shouldn't take too long for me to find a job. I'll find a job before school starts, and then I can pay you rent. I'll send in my final papers for school and get all my funding and loans set up. I've already looked into most of that so it shouldn't take too long. But I don't want to put you out before you go, since you probably have a lot of people to see and stuff."

None who matter as much as you, I think, but I keep that part to myself. "Tonight, you can come out with me and Silas and his girl Beth. We are meeting up with a few old friends for drinks, then I'll bring you back to your place and make sure he's gone. In the morning, I'll help you clear your place out."

Juliette half smiles and it kills me a little when the smile doesn't quite reach her eyes. She's here, though, and she's doing this.

"I probably stink. If we are going out, I need a shower. I'd kill for a bubble bath, but I'll take anything."

I grin. She's about to be one very, very happy girl. I grab her hand and lead her upstairs to my grandparents' bathroom, grabbing her duffel bag on the way. The house is older and it's been completely redone inside, but one thing that remains is a gigantic claw-foot tub. She gives a high-pitched squeal when she sees it, and I laugh out loud.

"I take it you like it? Thing's a huge pain to take a shower in," I say, and she almost violently pushes me back.

"What kind of monster takes a shower in this? You—you heathen!" she yells. By now, I'm laughing even harder.

"I'm a man, Juliette. I take manly showers. I don't bathe." She's barely listening to me; now she's over at the tub running her fingers along the rim. I'm immediately irrationally jealous of this tub.

"He doesn't mean it, baby. I'll make it up to you," she coos. Still chuckling, I turn to leave her to it.

"I'll be downstairs, tub-whisperer." I don't think she even notices when I close the door behind me. The reality that she's about to slide into that tub naked hits me, and I try to figure out a way I can get one of those tubs in my apartment, like yesterday. I take a few deep breaths and force myself to think about the last time I saw Gramps take his teeth out before I'm ready to go downstairs.

I grab an apple from the counter and head to the living room where my grandparents are sitting. When I came down to visit, I had immediately asked them if I could stay here, knowing they wouldn't mind. My mom is still here in town, but she's living with her guy of the week and I'd rather not get too close to that. Besides, my grandparents are the ones who came to see me when I got to my first posting, they're the ones who call once a week to check in, they likely know where I am if I've been tasked or deployed out somewhere at any given time. I doubt Mom has ever had a clue. Her support of me has always been made up entirely of her willingness to tell literally anyone who will listen about her hero son who serves his country, never mind that I haven't even been to Afghanistan yet or done anything worth celebrating. She's always been sure to use my job to garner sympathy and support for herself. She's just never funnelled any of that pride into caring in the slightest about how I am or what I'm doing.

Anyways, Grandma and Gramps feed me and I'll basically go anywhere for food.

My grandma looks up from her quilt table when she hears me come in the room. "Were you able to pick up your friend okay?" she asks. When I bolted after brunch, I told them I had a friend with an emergency who I needed to pick up. My mom had looked put out. The whole brunch had just been my way of agreeing to see her, and I think she'd been hoping I'd go visit people with her so her friends could fawn over me. Her boyfriend had mostly just looked hungover and annoyed at my existence, and it was clear Mom was only there to find out more about my deployment so she could use the whole military family deal to her advantage as much as she could. I was sorry I even told her I was leaving, and I wasn't sad I had to cut our meal short. My grandparents had just smiled and let me know I was welcome to bring her back with me if I needed to. Come to think of it, I'm not even sure how they knew it was a 'her.'

"I did. She's upstairs in the tub. Thanks for letting me bring her here. I'm going to take her back to her place tonight. We're going to meet Silas and Beth for the evening down at the Crown." Grandma just nods and gets back to her quilting. I look over at Gramps, but I realize that he's not actually watching the TV; he's fast asleep. I sit down on the couch beside him and turn the program up a bit to watch the game. I'm not really paying attention; I'm trying to wrap my head around my day so far.

I have Juliette here with me and no idea what I'm going to do with her.

Nine

Juliette

This tub is possibly heaven on Earth.

I can't remember the last time I had a bathtub where I could submerge my whole body. I close my eyes and let my head sink under the water so just my nose can peek out of the bubbles to breathe. It's so relaxing I can almost forget that I just changed my entire life in the last twenty-four hours.

It's not like I've never irrationally quit a job, or walked out on a guy, or done something equally as thoughtlessly spontaneous. But all those times I did it with the knowledge that I was still going to be... me. I was just going to find the same kind of job, the same kind of apartment, the same kind of guy. I was going to keep living the same kind of life. Same shit, different pile, like they say. I guess I never got that saying until now. This is different, though. If I leave with Tavish, I have to make a change. I was terrible at school as a kid. Would I be able to attend classes and work enough to pay him for the apartment? Where would I even work? All my job experience has been at bars and seedy clubs, but I don't think I'd last long working until two a.m. and then trying to get to class in the morning. I've already researched funding and I know I have a good chance of receiving the grants I applied for that would cover most of my tuition, and I could qualify for a student loan to help with the rest. Would it be enough though? What if I flunk out?

I applied for Media and Communications because the idea of one day having a real job in marketing both thrills and terrifies me. In the end, it's not like there's a lifetime career to be had in flashing my cleavage to drunk customers at trashy bars, so I might as well give it a try to be something more. Who knows, maybe I could go back to the bars as a manager or something. Anything would be better than working job to job with a time clock over my head, reminding me I'm getting older.

I spend a lot of time running it over and over in my head until eventually I have to accept that the water is getting cold and my body looks like a gigantic prune, so I empty the tub and dry off. I pull on some jeans and a t-shirt, and pull my hair back into a messy French braid. I even take the time for a bit of makeup, but I can't fix my lip. The skin below is turning a funny green. I hadn't realized how hard he'd hit me. After shoving all my things back in my duffel bag, I wipe down the beautiful tub and nervously walk downstairs.

"Tavish?" I call. I've never met his grandparents, probably because most of the time when Tavish and I have seen each other, it's been after midnight. Actually, *all* the time. I know he's close with them, though, and that he lived there at the end of high school. I'm really hoping they're okay with me being here. I turn the corner to see a smiling older woman sitting quilting at a table in the living room. Her hair is an odd shade of red that must come from a bottle at her age but I would never have guessed, and her eyes are the same liquid green as Tavish's.

"You must be Tavish's friend. I'm Rebecca. You'll have to forgive me for not getting up; there's thread everywhere right now." I smile and nod.

"Hi, I'm Juliette. Thank you so much for lending me your amazing bathtub. That was so relaxing. Have you seen..." I'm about to say Tavish's name until my eye catches him sitting on the couch with someone I assume is his grandfather. They are both in the same position: heads back, mouths open, eyes closed, fast asleep. I can't help but laugh.

"They've fallen asleep like that more times than I can count. Seems the excitement has worn poor Tavish right out. Why don't you make us both some tea, darling? The kettle is on the stove and the teabags are in the canister." I look back at Rebecca and smile. This woman just radiates hospitality. I love her already.

I head into the kitchen and put on the kettle, grabbing a couple mugs from where they sit drying by the sink. An old-fashioned white canister with the word "tea" scrolled across the front sits with several others like it on the worn, cream-coloured counter. This is the house Tavish lived in until he was in grade school and his mom decided she didn't want to live with her parents anymore. According to Tavish, they'd always been kind to him, parenting him far more than his mother ever did, but his mom didn't like the responsibility that they placed on her shoulders or the expectations that they had for her to get her act together once she had a child. So, she'd left and taken him with her, though he suspected she regretted not going alone. Tavish still spent much of his time here, even coming back to live as a teen when his mom moved in with some guy who apparently didn't want him around. Tavish didn't talk much about his mom, but he was always quick to share about his two grandparents. It was clear who had made the positive impressions in his life.

Heading back into the living room, I hand Rebecca her tea and sit on the recliner across from her. She looks up at me and suddenly I see her eyebrows knit for just one moment before she looks back down to her quilt.

"You know, when I was younger, it wasn't really considered all that wrong for a man to lay a hand on his woman," she begins, and I realize I'd forgotten about my green bruise and lip that is still puffy with a nice-looking split down the side. "But it was never okay, even when it was. It's funny how as women, we can pick apart every single imperfection in ourselves, but are so quick to make excuses to justify another's bad behaviour. I just met you, my dear, but you're worth more than that."

I have no idea what Tavish told his grandparents when he left brunch to come get me, but I'm sure it hadn't been much. No, I get the impression Rebecca sees something all on her own. I stare down at my cup, absently twisting the little paper at the end of the tea bag. I'm not sure what to say.

"I don't know if he mentioned it, but when Tavish was younger, finishing high school, he lived here at our place again after 10 years or so with his mom. It took some getting used to for him. He'd always been such a good kid, but his mom had never really had any rules for him as long as he stayed out of her way. When he asked to live with us, we worried that maybe one of his mom's boyfriends was getting violent. Then one night, he finally opened up to his grandfather with the truth: he'd only stayed with his mom all those years before *because* a lot of the boyfriends were violent in some way or another, and he didn't want to leave his mom alone with them. That boy learned to fight at a young age to protect his mother. Even knowing he could've walked away and come here years earlier, he only finally left when his mom didn't give him a choice and instead picked one of them over him."

Despite my tea, my throat is dry and the fingers I'm staring at in my lap look blurry. I open my mouth but nothing comes out. I had no idea.

"I only tell you this story because our Tavish, he's always been a bit rough, but he's a protector, not a fighter. Sometimes people don't realize there is a difference, but there is. A fighter looks for a reason to be violent, but a protector—a protector only raises his fists when the reason is brought to him. We realized then that the boy has always been strong willed, but those fights he was in were never because of his own pain. They were always to defend against someone else's. I worried for a few years when he was here, because he'd spend so many nights away from home, thinking his grandfather and I didn't notice. I was scared he was in over his head with something. Sometimes, when he'd come back, he'd look so defeated my heart broke for him. But then I'd remember that the boy is a protector, always has been, and wherever he was, I trusted he was doing what came best. I don't know what that was, but I do know that he was the right person for you to call."

My head is spinning, and I'm just about to ask if they knew I was the reason Tavish always snuck out, but right when I look up, I see Tavish out of the corner of my eye, awake and looking at me. I wonder for an instant how much of that he heard, but looking at his face, it's clear he heard it all. His eyes are almost pleading for a moment, like he's willing me not to make the connection between his grandmother's story and our own. All I can picture now is that little boy fighting to protect his mother.

"I'm sorry I interrupted your brunch, Rebecca. I know you and his grandfather must be eager to spend as much time as you can with him before…" Before he leaves. I've blocked that part out until now. Tavish is leaving for Afghanistan soon, and here I am, barrelling into his life with all my drama and garbage.

"Oh, that's not a problem, my dear. Don't worry yourself about that. The brunch was just a way for him to see his mother on his own terms, and I'm willing to bet he'd had more than enough by the time you called."

"Definitely," Tavish says from over on the couch. "I'll see Grandma and Gramps plenty before I'm gone. It wasn't a problem." He slowly stands up and stretches, his t-shirt pulling up above his belt line. I'm staring at that little strip of skin maybe a little too closely when he catches my eye. Crap. He just grins at me. Double crap. Now is definitely not the time for me to start wanting things I can't have. Who am I kidding? It wouldn't be the start, but it's still just as unreachable.

He puts his hand out and I realize I have a death grip on my now-empty tea mug. I pass it to him, but he switches it to the other hand and puts his hand back out to me. I grab it and he hauls me up, his fingers gently resting on my hips for just a moment to steady me on my feet.

"Silas and Beth will meet us at the pub in a half hour or so. You ready to go?" He looks at me like I'm breakable, and it's completely adorable. At her table, I can see Rebecca with a sly grin on her face. I'm suddenly both sure that Tavish never told her and positive that she knows it had been me stealing her grandson away in the night. It had always been me.

Tavish says the pub isn't far, which means we can walk, and by the time we're halfway down the street in comfortable silence, I'm lost in my own head. It has never occurred to me what our friendship looks like from the other side. How many times had Rebecca watched her grandson chase me down in the night? How selfish must I have seemed, to send him back each time looking so hopeless? I wasn't a friend, I was a burden. We had never gone to the movies, hung out with each other's friends or family, never gone shopping together, never even been inside each other's homes. I'd just lived my life and Tavish had caught me when I fell, only to set me back up and watch me go back out each time.

How many times had I been the one to call? I don't even remember ever calling him. My heart knows deep down there have been times I must have, times I dialled his number late in the night because I needed someone. When I was too far gone to stand up straight, it seemed his was the first number I'd try. But had I ever called him sober? Had I ever called him to see how *he* was doing? Even once?

I hadn't been any kind of friend to Tavish, I'd been a responsibility. A heavy one at that.

It takes me a moment to realize we've stopped walking and Tavish is standing in front of me, crouched lower and looking up to catch my eyes. He seems to do this a lot, putting himself at eye level instead of making me look up at him. I see that shade of green again for the first time, that colour that looks like it belongs on a beach instead of staring at me. He's skipping from one eye to another, searching. Not for the first time I really wonder what he sees that has kept him tied to me.

"Did you know this is the first time we've ever seen each other in the light of day? I've been a terrible friend, Tavish," I whisper to him. He stands up straight and grabs me by the back of my head roughly, pulling me into his chest.

"I never asked you to be my friend, Jules. I promised that I'd be *your* friend. I never asked you to do anything but let me."

I almost wish he'd have lied to me, just told me that I was too hard on myself and I really had been a good friend. He didn't, though. It's not like there is an excuse for my bad behaviour. No "it's okay, you were going through a hard time," because we both know the truth. I was a terrible friend because I made terrible choices. For years. There is nothing more to it than that. Did I even give him the chance to judge me for himself? I never even told him why I made the choices I did and he never asked.

I want to tell him I don't deserve it. I want to yell at him for trusting me, for being so naive that he'd stick with me. Then I remember that I haven't seen him in five years. Maybe he did give up. It makes sense that it would've been the right time for him to just cut his losses and move on. So why is he back now if I wasn't worth it then? I realize that it's the most selfish thing that it bothers me now, after I've just understood what a horrible person I've been, but it does. I want to know what happened. I want to know why he's here.

"You never called after you left. I figured now that you were grown up, you'd given up on me. That you finally realized I wasn't worth it. And I'm not. Fuck, Tavish, you were right to go and not look back. So why are you back now?" Tavish visibly cringes. His face is pained, as though he possibly could be blamed for walking away from me. He had every right to. I was never worth him. I just don't know why he's here now.

"Jules—" Suddenly, his phone rings in his pocket. He pulls it out and glances at the screen, then flips it open fast. "Cleary." His voice is different. Official sounding. He listens for a moment and his face changes. "I'm in Calgary, but I can be there tomorrow." He laughs for a moment. "Yes, Sarge, I'm with Corporal Jameson, as usual. I'll let him know." When he closes his phone, he just stares at it a moment.

"Our dates have changed. We report day after tomorrow."

Ten

Tavish

This isn't the first time the Army has messed with my plans. Changing the date by five days isn't the strangest thing that's ever happened, but man. This timing sucks.

Poor Juliette. If I was surprised, then she was shocked. She's never had the chance to know that this is just how the military works. I spend some time reassuring her our plan will still work. Hell, I'm reassuring both of us while I talk. In the morning, we'll just have to pack her up as quickly as we can and she can come up with me tomorrow night. I don't admit I'd already called my roommate yesterday and told him to let his girlfriend and the landlord know she was coming. She doesn't need to know how confident I was that I could convince her to let me help look after her.

Once I'm sure she understands, we head inside the pub. Silas and Beth are already sitting at a booth in the back with a couple of other friends. I introduce Juliette to Beth and catch Silas' eye. I'm pretty sure he already knows what's up before we walk out by the bathrooms and I let him know.

"Fuck." I swear Silas can turn that word into as many syllables as he wants; it's almost a gift. He slowly drags his hands down his face like he always does when he's trying to think something through. "Beth isn't going to be happy. She'll get it, but she's not going to like it. At all."

With Beth in the picture, Silas and I live very different lives. Even though we are almost always together, we are nothing alike. On the outside, we seem similar: his hair is a little blonder, his eyes are blue instead of green and he's a little bit shorter, but we've been told we have the same look to us and I guess I see it. After a drunken decision on a R&R in Europe, we even have the same tattoo on our chests, a regimental crest. That's where the similarity ends, though. He's so much more relaxed, little seems to really faze him. He rarely makes a rash decision, always the voice of reason to my emotionally driven behaviour. Truth is, without the military, I doubt we'd have even really gotten along, but there's something about serving with someone that makes us brothers, regardless. Since our first day of Basic Training, we've been on every course, every deployment, every exercise together. I suppose it could've gone either way, we might have grown to resent each other. Instead, we just fell in step together. We fight with each other all the time but we fight *for* each other more. He's the closest I have to a brother. I guess that's how the sergeant knew when he called that I was with Silas. I always am.

Silas and Beth were engaged before he even left for Basic Training with me, but they're still not married. They apparently met in their first year of college and stayed together, even after Silas decided school wasn't for him and started working at a warehouse. I used to wonder why he didn't just enlist right away when he left college, but I have the feeling he didn't want Beth to know he put it off so he could keep supporting her until she finished. He proposed at her graduation and left soon after for the military. When we first got posted, he and I moved in together while Beth wrapped things up back home. Eventually, she moved up with him and I found a new roommate.

Beth is much more tightly wound than Silas is, but I think everyone would look tense next to him. I've never seen the guy lose his cool. She graduated with a degree in business, and I know she works as a manager at some upscale shop downtown. She's pretty, something that's more just a statement of fact to me than a real concept, for as long as I've known her she's been Silas' girl and that makes her more of a sister to me than anything. While his colouring is light, hers is dark. Her skin is olive, and I'm sure someone in her family must be Asian somewhere down the line, but she never talks about them. Her family is in Vancouver and I get the feeling they don't spend time together, and the only family I've ever seen them visit is his. Her black hair is thick and long. She tries all the time to wear it down, but by the end of the night, it's almost always up on top of her head, held by pencils, chopsticks, and once I saw her use a couple straws at a restaurant. Where Silas has tattoos covering every inch of skin the Army allows, Beth's skin is blank. She's taller than Juliette and Silas is shorter than I am, but she still fits under his chin.

It seems strange that they aren't married yet. He says they're not in a hurry, but I think it might be because Silas has a very specific idea in his head about what marriage looks like. He wants to give her a bigger house and a two-car garage, money for vacations and college funds for kids. He wants to give her the white picket fence and everything that goes with it. Truth is, I don't think Beth gives a single care about any of it. She just wants him. She thinks *he's* the one who needs all that. It's funny that they seem to know everything about each other, but neither is willing to admit they're both waiting, thinking that the other isn't ready. Maybe neither of them are.

Silas and I stand and talk through the logistics of grabbing our gear and getting it and ourselves to the base. He and Beth will leave tomorrow morning. I let him know I'll be there mid-afternoon once I have Juliette all packed up, and he offers to stop by her place in the morning on his way to pick up some of her things since I'm on my bike. He gives me some curious looks but he doesn't say anything. I'm guessing he figures he'll have six months to ask me all the questions he wants. Eventually, we've put it off long enough, and we head back to the table so he can talk it over with Beth.

She and Juliette are chatting away, but it's forced. I know they'll get along great, but right now Jules is trying not to say anything and I know Beth is worried about what Silas and I were just discussing. She's been part of this life just as long as we have. She knows the score. Silas puts a hand on her shoulder and she gets up, walking silently with him to that same spot down the hall while I slide into the booth next to Jules. We both have our eyes glued to the two of them; it's impossible to look away. I see the exact moment she knows that she's lost the days she thought she'd have with him before we were gone.

I force myself to stop staring at them and look at Juliette. I can see the moisture in her eyes while she watches them. Her entire face radiates compassion and my heart squeezes in my chest. I've never so badly wanted to protect another person. I bet right now she thinks she looks terrible with her hair barely holding onto that braid that's pulling it back and her old t-shirt and jeans on. She always feels like she only looks good if she's trying, but I think she looks so much better when she's not. When we were younger, I always saw her at the end of the night, when her makeup was faded to nothing and her hair a mess. Hell, I've seen her with puke on her shirt and her shoes in her purse. I can't think of a time that I didn't think she looked beautiful. Without thinking, I reach out and loop my fingers around a piece of her hair that's fallen in front of her ear. Her breath catches for a moment, but she doesn't move. I hope so much it's because she doesn't want me to stop.

We sit there for a while, me looking at her while she gazes down the hall, and I twist her hair. Neither of us seems to know what to say, so I'm content to say nothing and just watch her. After several minutes, I glance quickly back up to Silas and Beth. He has his forehead down resting on hers and he's holding her hand, fingering her engagement ring while they quietly talk. Eventually, they walk back over to us and take a seat in the booth. Beth's face is lined, but she's not crying. I knew she wouldn't, not now. She will later, when it's just the two of them. This isn't the first time something like this has happened and I'm sure it won't be the last.

Beth is the first to break the silence. "Tavish, I know you were planning on finding some tropical resort to lounge on for your HLTA like you did for Bosnia, but what do you say we try to swing it so you come back here for it?" I look at her confused. Why would I come back to Canada for my mid-deployment leave? Especially when Thailand has beaches... I glance at Juliette. I guess I could be convinced.

"Seems someone has decided he's finally willing to marry me. As soon as this is over. Maybe sooner, if you guys can get an HLTA together."

I'm already standing up to congratulate them when Silas beats me to his feet. "And Cleary, that's because I need you there, to be my best man." He looks at me like he expects me to agree, as though it was even a question. I've already forgiven him for making me reconsider my beach plans. These two deserve this and he knows that if the Army lets me, I'll always be anywhere he needs me to be.

I give him the manliest hug we can manage and Juliette looks over to Beth in wonder. "Wow! That's so soon. You'll do all the planning yourself?"

"Ha! Soon... We've been engaged for so long I think everyone forgot that it happened! If it wasn't for the ring, I probably would've, too... It's time, though. It won't be big. Just some family and our close friends. I don't know when I'll get confirmation of his time home so I might have to pull the whole thing together in a matter of weeks, but that's okay. We don't need anything fancy. If Tavish can come home with him on HLTA, we'll plan for then; otherwise, right when they get back. I don't mind a winter wedding. I've always wanted a dress with a furry muff."

I stifle my laugh. I don't know what a muff is, but I'm betting it's not what it sounds like to me. Silas smirks at me, he knows where my head is. Beth beams up at him and my heart squeezes in my chest. I've always been happy to be able to leave whenever I need for wherever I'm told without the worry of anyone at home, but for maybe the first time I find myself wanting what they have. I flag our waitress and let her know the good news when I order a round of beer for the two of us and a bottle of champagne for the girls. She looks at me a little funny, I doubt they get many requests for champagne in this pub, but she promises she'll find some in the back.

"Have you been a best man before, Slick?" Jules asks, looking at me, and I open my mouth to respond only to be cut off by Silas.

"Slick? SLICK? Oh man! That's the best! Why Slick, Juliette? He's never told me about this." Shit.

"Really?" Juliette looks at me with mischief in her eyes, and I know I'm sunk. I just lean back on the bench with my beer and accept my fate.

"Well, when Tavish and I first met, we were seventeen and I was walking home from work after midnight. He pulled up on his motorcycle and basically demanded like some caveman that I get on the back so he could *drive me home*." She says the last three words in the most suggestive way she can muster and Silas is killing himself laughing.

"Turns out he actually did just drive me home. We talked on the phone that whole night and we've been friends ever since." Silas gives me a look at the word "friends," but I just slightly shake my head for him to let it go. "But I realized then that it had all been way out of character for him. Tavish isn't smooth. At all. Picking up a girl he doesn't know on the side of the road is not his style, at least it definitely wasn't then, so the name stuck. I'm sure I'm the only one who calls him that."

That's where I cut it. "For one, yes, yes, she is. The *only* one. So, don't even think about it. For two, it wasn't just after midnight; it was the middle of the fucking night and she was a tiny girl by herself in half a shirt. I didn't want her to get hurt. And three, you make it sound like I can't pick up a girl, Jules. I'm clearly really good at it. I got you on my bike, didn't I?"

Jules just smiles at me, and Silas is still laughing. I have a feeling this is going to haunt me for a while, especially since we've got nothing but time together the next six months. Silas' laughter is only the beginning of what I'm going to hear from the rest of the guys when he tells them.

The evening passes quickly. Juliette and Beth finish their bottle of champagne and start on the wine while they get more and more animated, discussing wedding plans, house decor and Juliette's schooling. It's great to see. Beth doesn't have a lot of friends at home; when she moved up with Silas none of the guys had any significant others, at least none that stuck around. She was usually the odd girl out when we'd go out as a group, or she'd be stuck with whatever girl I or one of the other guys dragged along. I'll be the first to admit none of those girls had much to offer in terms of friendship for her. We tend to stick pretty low-bar. My roommate Jason started dating someone seriously a while ago, but she doesn't seem to connect with her either, not like she is now with Juliette. I love watching her make a friend. She's excited to hear Juliette is coming up to my place and encourages her with her school plans. She and Juliette are soon planning away for the possibility of a wedding when we get back on leave, and for some reason there are a lot of balloons involved. Turns out Beth has a thing for balloons. Who knew?

I'm just about to explain to Jules that as much as I'll try, there's a good chance the Army won't let us both home at the same time, but Beth explains it all to her better than I ever could. If the Army won't give us leave together, the wedding will just have to wait until we're home for good. Listening to Beth explain the ins and outs of the unpredictable military to a completely clueless Juliette is reassuring. I don't know what Jules and I are right now, but no matter what the status of our relationship is, she'll be home while I'll be gone. I've thrown her in blind, and she'll need someone who knows how to navigate all that will come with it. Silas and I just let them talk while we sit there and nurse our beers. Neither of us feels much like drinking and we're both happy to see the two ladies connect, knowing the year they have ahead.

Friends come in and out, saying hi. I haven't kept in touch with many people from here. I was only just out of high school when I left and didn't have a lot tying me to "home" other than holiday trips to see my grandparents. Silas and Beth have more connections from work and university. Most people seem awkward around us, and more than once, we are so caught up in the four of us we lose track of when others leave. It's interesting and a little isolating the way military life provides you with a whole other family but at the same time often seems to disconnect you from the friends you had before.

It's nearing midnight when we head back home; early still, but we have a big day tomorrow. Beth and Juliette exchange numbers, and she and I walk back to my grandparents' house to grab my bike. Juliette's a little wobbly. She had far more to drink than I since I knew I was driving, but she also has a lot of experience holding her liquor. I think she'd probably be able to drink both Silas and me under the table, but I keep that to myself. I don't need to give the guys any more ammo to rib me about, and being out-drunk by a tiny girl like Jules is definitely something they'd find funny. She's a little giggly, though, and I don't blame her for blowing off some steam. Her whole life changed today. Essentially, she's running away with me tomorrow, and I just told her I'll leave the next day. That's a lot to take in.

We pull up to her apartment building and slowly make our way up the stairs. When we get to the door, I grab the key from her hand and open it myself, pressing her behind me. I'm already wound up just walking in. If that jerk is here, it's not going to be pretty—for him, at least. If he's on his own, I got this, but I know Silas isn't too far away if he's decided to call some friends. Not to sound cocky, but even if he has, if they're anything like him, I'm still probably fine on my own. I'd like to knock the fucker around but for Juliette's sake, I'm hoping for quiet.

It's dark inside and I do a quick run through of the four rooms before I let her in. There's no one around. Turns out, this moving-out thing might be easier than I thought. At least, I hope she sees it that way.

"Son of a bitch," I mutter as I flip the light and let Juliette in. There's literally nothing left in the apartment but some broken bits of a table and a bunch of garbage. Now I realize why Jules wanted to come back here before he left to make sure she had her own things. The fucker took everything. Even the cupboards are empty.

I keep my eyes on her to gauge her reaction. She doesn't even look a little bit surprised, just resigned. She walks down the hall silently and glances into the bedroom and bathroom. "Well," she says, "I guess I just have some cleaning up to do. Moving out will be pretty easy after all." She forces herself to smile up at me, God, even faced with this mess she's stunning. I walk over and wrap my arms around her. I keep waiting for something to break, but she's always stronger than I think she'll be.

"We'll grab some cleaning supplies from my grandparents' place and come back in the morning," I tell her. "Now's not the time to worry about this. Are you okay?"

She just laughs a little. "Everything in here was crap. The bed, the couch, the TV. It was all hand-me-down garbage from friends or from second-hand stores. You were here, we didn't have much; we even only had two sets of dishes. I took everything I really needed. When the time comes for me to get my own place, I'll just have to scrounge again. This," she gestures to the room, "wasn't the first time I've started over. Stuff like that is all easily replaced, and surprisingly, it doesn't look like he trashed the place too bad. I should be able to get my damage deposit back."

I grab her hand and start towards the door, but she plants her feet and looks at me puzzled.

"I'll be fine here tidying up tonight, and I can grab a nap once I'm done. Just give me a call when you get up in the morning, and I'll let you know when I've finished up here." She's not even looking at me while she talks, just surveying the damage. I think she might be mentally preparing herself to sleep on the carpet. Besides the fact that I'd never let that happen, what if that twat came back while she's here alone? I'd already planned to crash on the couch to watch over her, but seeing this? Not a chance she's staying here.

Without thinking it through, I stride over to her and scoop her up in my arms like a doll, grabbing my helmet from the counter and clumsily locking the door behind me as we leave. "Where are we going?" she shrieks. "You can't just take me back to your grandparents' house! I'll be fine here."

"I could, and they'd be fine with it, but I'm not going to. And you'd be fine here, I'm sure, because you're a strong girl, but I'm not leaving you here either." I carry her down the stairs and out to the street before I put her down. "Get on the bike, Jules."

She just looks at me and does what I say. I both love and hate how easily she follows direction. It scares me how fast she might listen to someone who's not me. I try not to think about how many times she already has. I drive for a while before I realize I don't really know where I'm going, but eventually pull up at a hotel not too far away.

"Tavish, this is silly. It's already after midnight and I can sleep on the carpet for one night."

"You can, but you won't. Wait here." I head inside, and I'm grateful that this is the kind of place that doesn't give me a second look for checking in this late. Thankfully, they have a room available with two double beds. I head back and grab Jules and my backpack. I'd only packed overnight things for her, but thanks to the Army and a whole lot of travelling, I always have an extra pair of boxers and socks in my bag. It won't kill me to wear the same jeans and t-shirt tomorrow. I'd already figured I was sleeping in my clothes on the couch. We get up to our room, and I toss the backpack on the ground before I look at her. I can tell before she even meets my eye. She may be standing in the room with me, but she's already gone.

She's not my Jules right now. She's the Juliette that thinks she knows what I expect when I bring her to a hotel. And that Jules has already buried her heart so that she can give everything but it away. It's like it hasn't occurred to her that she has a choice, and because of that, she doesn't. I can't believe she still thinks I'd take that from her. I can't. I won't. Not when she looks at me like that.

I peek into the bathroom at the tub and decide. From my backpack, I grab a flashlight and set it on the sink. I turn it on and leave the bathroom light off, the closest to candlelight I can get. Then I take the hotel body wash from the counter and pour it under the tap while I run hot water. As the water runs, I empty out my bag and show Juliette the extra clothes to remind her she has something to change into. Then keeping my eye on her, I strip down. My body feels like it's on fire, the material of my jeans scrapes on my skin as I pull them down and kick them to the side with my shirt. Standing there staring at her in my boxer briefs, I finally drop my eyes and hop into the tub quickly before my body makes this more embarrassing than it needs to be.

"Come."

She looks at me for a moment and I wish I thought that leaving my boxers on made it easier for her, but I know that's not true. She doesn't know what to do now, in this room, if I take sex off the table. This is outside the box for her, and I can practically hear her thoughts.

"Stop thinking. Come."

She shakes her head and pulls her shirt off. I keep my eyes fixed on hers, both to send her a message that this is safe and to keep myself under control. She's stunning, and as she bends slightly to unbutton her jeans and shimmy out of them, it takes every ounce of self-control I have to not jump out of the tub and taste every inch of her.

She's smattered in tattoos, all the way up one arm and across her chest, of colourful flowers and skulls. Peeking under her bra is another tattoo tracing the lines under her breasts across her ribcage. There's more on her legs, words circling what I think are butterflies. I've seen the wings on her shoulders, and I can see now that they go all the way down her back past her hips. Her body is tiny but soft. I think she'd say that's a flaw, but it's a beautiful soft, the kind you want to bury yourself in.

I do my very best to control my features and look at her eyes without the abject want that is pressing down on me. I'm thankful for the bubbles that have taken over the tub, hiding what she does to me. The look on her face changes as she stands there for a moment in her bra and panties. She almost looks hurt before she turns her back and slowly dips herself into the water in front of me. The tub is thankfully bigger than average, but it's still a tight fit with the two of us. At six foot two, I'm not the biggest guy around, but I'm not small either. Thankfully Juliette is. Still, she looks pained, sitting awkwardly in front of me, trying not to touch my torso. It occurs to me that I'm so worried about her thinking that it's the only thing I want that I haven't considered how she'd feel if she thinks I don't want it at all.

I slide my hands to her side and jerk her back, splashing some water onto the tile. She makes a little squeaky noise and stiffens for a minute, no doubt feeling what I can't control pushing against her lower back. I unsuccessfully try to stifle a moan at the touch. She finally relaxes and lets her body lean back against my chest, her head just under my chin.

"Never doubt how beautiful you are, Jules. Or how much I want you. It's just not the right time." She lets out a breath and closes her eyes.

"I thought you were too manly to bathe, Slick," she murmurs.

"Not with you I'm not."

The two of us lie there in silence for a long time. At one point, I even reach with my toes and turn the tap back on to add more hot water when it starts to cool. Eventually, I feel her body relax completely on me, her head falls a little and I can feel her slow breath on my shoulder. I pull my legs underneath me and as delicately as I can manage stand while scooping her up. I grab a towel from the rack and wrap her up in it. She's so tiny. I love the way she fits in my arms.

She's still mostly asleep when I set her down on one of the beds. I try gently to wake her, but she's out. After the day she's had, I'm not surprised, and I'm sure all that champagne and wine didn't help. I look at her for a long while, and I know I must get her out of the wet bra and panties she has on. I could strip her down right now and she probably wouldn't even remember, but I'm already testing the limits of my resolve tonight. I decide on my best bet and grab my t-shirt, pulling it over her. Once it's on, I reach my hands under her back and unhook her bra, pulling it out. I do my best to cover her while I try to wrestle her sopping wet panties off. Forget the stupid peacekeeping medal, I should get one for managing to keep my hands to myself tonight.

By the time I crawl into the other bed in dry boxers, it's well after two a.m. I should be exhausted, but I lie there for a long time staring at her from across the room, listening to her breathing. I've watched her sleep before, late nights at Denny's while she comes down, and Juliette and I've even fallen asleep together, usually outside at a park while we waited until she could go home. It's never been like this, though. In a bed, just the two of us and no distractions.

"Slick." Her eyes are still closed and her speech is a little slurred with sleep, but I hear her call me. I doubt she's even completely awake.

"Yeah?"

"I hate you over there. Come lie with me. Please."

She has no idea how badly I want to, but I promised myself that I wouldn't touch her and falling asleep with her pressing against me isn't going to make that any easier. I can't say no to her, though, so I slip into the bed next to her and lie there without touching her, staring at the ceiling. After a couple of minutes, she rolls over and tucks her head under my arm, resting it on my chest and clinging against my side, one arm across my stomach. She feels perfect. I exhale a breath I didn't even know I was holding and let my arm fall around her shoulders before I close my eyes and let myself drift off.

She's here. With me. On me.

She's **here.**

Only problem is I'm leaving for half a year and I can't deny my selfish need for her to be here when I get back.

I've either fixed everything or ruined it all. I wish I knew which.

ALL THE WAY HOME

Eleven

Juliette

I wake up to a mouthful of cotton balls and an empty bed.

It takes me awhile to remember where I am before I see Tavish saunter out from the bathroom with a carafe of water in his hand to pour in the coffee maker. His jeans are back on, low on his hips. He hasn't put his belt back on, or his shirt. Oh. Tavish has grown up, and it looks good on him. Really, really good. That's about when I realize he's not wearing a shirt because I'm wearing it. And... nothing else. Dammit. I don't remember that happening. I suddenly feel sick, and it's not the faint hangover. I didn't think I drank that much, but the last thing I really remember is falling asleep with him in the bathtub. I wouldn't have... ha. Of course, I would. *He* wouldn't have though... would he? I take a quick glance at the other bed. It looks like someone was there at least at some point, but I'm sure I remember him next to me in the night.

Tavish looks over at me and must have noticed the look on my face, because he puts down the carafe and sits next to me on the bed, passing me a glass of water. "Jules, I swear I didn't look. You were wet, so I put my shirt on you and then took your wet stuff off so I couldn't see. I promise. You asked me to lie down with you, so I did, but that's all. Honest." The way he's looking at me kills me. No guy has ever looked like that, as though it would've been his fault if he touched me when I'm the one who drank too much wine and fell asleep in my wet underwear. Looking in his eyes, it's like he reads my mind.

"Jules, if I'd touched you and you couldn't even remember, that would've been entirely my fault. Do you get that? You didn't pass out, Jules, you didn't drink that much, you were just exhausted and fell asleep. Even if you'd passed out, it still would not be your fault. Ever. It's important to me that you know that I'd never take advantage like that." He looks so sincere, I don't even know how to answer him.

"You're the best person I've ever met, do you know that?" It's all I can think of to say.

"Only because you hang out with assholes, Jules. C'mon, we need to get that place of yours cleaned up. I want to get you settled in at my place as soon as I can."

He goes to stand up, but I grab his arm and trace my hand over his tattoo, that first one I saw way back before he left. He's got quite a few more now. There's a symbol over his heart on his chest that looks like it's something military. There's an almost tribal design snaked down his other shoulder to his elbow, and that whole arm is filled in with colour. On this arm, though, it's just one pin-up girl on the bike.

"She—" I start, but he gives a deep sigh, like he's preparing himself for something, and cuts me off.

"I drew her. Or you, I guess that's obvious. That first night I saw you, when we were talking on the phone, I drew you. That's why it's my old bike. I really liked it, so I had it done when I turned eighteen." It's beautiful, with simple lines, and the girl is looking back at me with full pink lips and huge brown eyes. There's no mistaking it's me. She looks just like me, in a cartoon way. For a pin-up girl, though, she's not just sexy. She looks softer, innocent. Nothing like me. I look at the bike, and it has the word "Faithful" scrawled across the tank. His bike had been just flat black.

"Why 'Faithful?'" This time Tavish pulls away and stands.

"It's nothing, Jules. Just thought it'd look better with something on there."

I stand up right in front of him, suddenly aware that his shirt isn't *that* long on me. I'm not backing down, though.

"No. I don't think that's it." My voice is just a whisper, but I'm so close to him, it doesn't matter.

"What do you want me to say, Jules? That it was a promise? That I told myself that I was going to look out for you forever, no matter what, and then I left and I realized I would never be good enough to convince you to let me rescue you, so I gave up? That now it just torments me? That every time I'm with someone else now I see it like a reminder that I'm only with them because I couldn't get to you? Is that what you want me to say?" His voice is pained but quiet, a whisper from just above my ear. I take a step back, no longer caring about my tiny shirt dress, so I can see his face. His eyes are closed, his head bowed. The light where the curtains are joined at the window casts a line of sunlight across the definition of his chest. His hands are by his sides, his fists opening and closing, tensing the muscles in his forearms and for a moment, I'm completely mesmerized by the smatter of freckles on his shoulders, by the lines of his stomach, by... him.

"Look at me," I plead. He takes a shaky breath and pauses the longest moment before he opens his eyes. The liquid green pierces as he stares down at me.

"Jules, it's okay... really. I'm sorry I—" Before he can finish, I rise up on my toes and press my lips on his. His whole body freezes for a minute, and I think he might push me away but instead he shudders. Suddenly, his hand is fisted in my hair, pulling my head up, pressing me against him, and even though I started this, there's no mistaking that now he's the one in control. I'm taken back to that moment before he left, at the abandoned building. The fierce possession in his kiss hasn't changed. His other hand doesn't move from my hip, holding tight but not pulling me any closer. He's entirely focused just on kissing me. Never has anyone kissed me like that. I always thought it was just something guys used as a means to an end, but this, this is amazing. He tastes like mint, and I almost forget I just woke up and haven't even brushed my teeth.

After what seems like a glorious forever, he drops his hand from my hair and steps back. As soon as his warmth is gone, I shiver and sit back on the edge of the bed. Tavish yanks the blanket off the bed in one motion and drapes it over my shoulders before kneeling on the floor in front of me.

"Jules." He searches my eyes for a minute, and I try with all I am to show him how I feel, even though I feel as lost as he looks. "I don't... I don't know what I should do right now." His tone is almost resigned, like he thinks he knows what he *should* do, but that's not what he *wants* to do. I'm still dazed. Did he say he didn't think he was good enough for me? Does he understand I'm the broken one? I have nothing to offer him, especially when he's shown over and over he doesn't want the one thing I'm good at giving up, the part of me that's already been used up. He doesn't want someone like me.

"Slick, I don't understand. If you think you weren't a good enough friend, you're crazy. You were always there for me, and I never deserved it. When you left for the Army... no one expected you to be there forever, Tavish. I knew you wouldn't always be there to drive me home, and I never expected you to be. And you know what? You're here now. You're the only friend who is. Doesn't that tell you something? You've nothing to feel bad about."

"Jules, I'd have driven you home every damn day if I thought that would change your mind and one of those days you'd have just stayed with me." His eyes are red now and I just want to do something, anything, to take that look off his face.

"I'd have given you everything that very first night, Slick, but you didn't want me. I'm not the kind of girl that someone wants forever, and I know you didn't want to be with me like that when you knew where I'd been. I don't blame you. You deserve better."

"No. Dammit, Jules, is that really what you think? That I didn't want you? Every minute I was with you I wanted you. From the moment I saw you, I wanted you. Of course, I did. But I don't only want you like that, that way you give yourself to whoever asks. I want more. I want you to see me when you touch me. I want you to be with me without shutting down. I was never going to have that if I let myself just take you before you could give it all to me.

"I can see, in your eyes, when you shut down. You don't even know you do it, I don't think you ever see them, all the rest of them. I saw them. Do you know how many times you called me, Jules? Do you know how many times I picked you up? How many times I talked you down? How many times I put you back together? God, Jules, some nights I could see... they'd leave you there, you know, at some park, at some party, on some couch. You'd get up to walk to me and I'd see sometimes, down your leg in those tiny skirts..." His voice catches and he squeezes his eyes shut, his hands are clenched so hard now his knuckles are white and his forearms shake.

My face is wet and it takes me a minute to realize I'm crying. I don't even remember the last time that happened. Why is he doing this? No, that's not the right question. Why did he do it? He's right, I barely remember those times. I remember the consequences of them, though. All those morning trips downtown for pills to make it go away, as though swallowing pills could erase what I'd done. By the time I graduated high school, after one too many scares, I committed to being smarter about it. To be honest, I'm surprised I had no long-term damage or disease. After that I was always safe, but I was too far gone to be any more than that. Ever since that first time, it was like I couldn't give it away enough. Maybe I thought there would be one time I'd give it and I wouldn't get it back. Then I could be done with it.

All I can think is this is such a painful way for him to explain why he can't be with me, why I'm never going to be right for him.

"Juliette." He opens his eyes and tips my chin back up to look at him. "I'm not telling you this because I want to shame you, or hurt you. I want you to understand. I saw that you'd give that part of you to anyone. I don't know why you don't know your worth, but that's just the way it was. I waited because I didn't want to be just anyone to you, Juliette. I'm sorry... I'm screwing this up, and it's the worst possible way to explain how I love you."

What? What did he just say? I drop my chin when he lets go, still crying. I can't manage to say anything except, "How?"

"How do I love you? Desperately, Jules. Desperately and terribly and fiercely. Not like a brother, like I was supposed to. I tried, I really did, but I fell so hard it broke me. Five years I tried to let you go because I'm not supposed to fall in love with someone as young as we were, and I knew I couldn't make you be with me anyways, but I'm selfish, Juliette, and I couldn't stay away. So now I'm here, and I didn't plan this, especially when I leave tomorrow, but you're here. This happened, I'm not even sure how, but I guess now you know. It's been a long time, but I've always loved you and seeing you again, I already know that won't ever change."

As soon as the words are out of his mouth, he stands and walks back to the coffee maker, methodically pouring the water and the grounds without looking back. I want to say something. I need to say something.

"Tavish, I didn't know." That's not at all what I want to say, but it's all that comes out.

"I know, Jules. I didn't want you to know. You needed a friend. You need a friend. It's okay. It doesn't change anything. We're going to get you up to my place for school and I'm going to leave tomorrow. Let's just focus on that." He turns to pass me a cup of coffee but I just stare at him, stunned.

"Slick, you were the best friend I ever had. Look at me! I needed you again after five years, and you're here, rescuing me. No one has ever treated me like you did, like you are now. I've never deserved you." Tavish just smiles this time and then pulls me in for a hug, burying his face in my hair so I can feel his breath on the top of my head. I swear it feels like he's trying to breathe all of me into him.

"You'll always have me, Juliette. Now, let's get ready and get started; it's going to be a long day."

My mind is reeling and I'm completely stunned, but Tavish seems to be focused on just getting us to Edmonton and so I try to keep up, I get dressed and we drive back to his grandparents' place where Silas and Beth meet us. They grab my duffel bag to take up to Edmonton with them since it won't fit on the back of the bike. The easy friendship between Silas and Tavish amazes me. They just take care of what the other needs, no questions, like they just know the other one would do the same every time. Tavish is worried about me making the trip on his bike since it's almost four hours, so they offer to drive me up. I don't want to lose any time with Tavish, so I convince him to let me brave the trip. Once we say our goodbyes to those two, it's just us with Tavish's grandparents, and I feel very out of place.

Grandma hugs me first, as though she'll miss me, too. I just met her yesterday.

"You'll do great things, young lady. I'm so glad you're around for him right now." I'm not sure what she thinks I'll do, since he leaves in the morning. I guess keeping his bed warm while he's away is something, but only barely and far more for me than him. She turns to Tavish and presses her palms on his cheeks.

"You are loved, Tavish; above all, remember that you're loved." He gives her a hug but his eyes are on his Gramps, who is watching him from the next room. When he peels himself from Grandma, Gramps walks over to him, his eyes fixed and a grim look on his face.

"I've been to war, son. It's nothing like they told me it would be. Just keep your head down and come home."

Tavish grins and wraps his grandfather in his arms. "I'll be back, Gramps. I love you guys."

We're on the back of the bike before there's the chance it might get emotional. I ask Tavish if we're going to see his mom, but he just purses his lips and shakes his head. I decide I'm not going to push. I'm not one to talk; we're not going to my parents' place, either.

We spend the rest of the morning cleaning up my apartment. Once we bag all the garbage, there's not that much to do. I borrow a vacuum from the neighbour, and Tavish washes floors and cleans out the appliances that we hardly ever used anyways. I head to the landlord's house across the street. My place is just one of four in a building she owns, and it turns out she's happy I'm gone. She has a nephew she's been hoping to move in there so this will give her the opportunity. After a quick walk-through, she writes me a cheque for my damage deposit, and Tavish and I are on our way. An entire chapter of my life, cleaned in a few hours and left with the keys on the landlord's kitchen table. I don't even look back.

I decide to grab my headphones from my bag and plug my iPod in for the ride. I grew up riding on the back of my dad's bike. When I was younger and we had still gotten along, he used to take me for rides out to the mountains on the weekend. We'd meet some of his friends, and he'd buy me a Coke while they had beer and talked shop. My dad had rarely been home, and his biker friends had taken most of the time he wasn't working, so I'd treasured those times together as a kid. Once I grew into a rebellious teen, though, Dad just wanted to bury his head in the sand and continue to pretend to all his friends that I was the perfect angel. I suppose that's easier than the embarrassment of telling them at a dinner party that she's got a nasty drug habit and even worse, she's a slut. Mom and Dad stopped challenging the lies I told them about where I went or what I did, content to believe it all as long as I didn't embarrass them or force them to confront the truth. My dad even got me one of the first cell phones, so my mom could call to know I was okay, and I could tell them I was wherever I wanted them to think I was. We all knew they wanted to believe the lie as much as I wanted to tell it. Very soon after I finished high school, I was gone. They made it clear they didn't want to know what I was doing and as the years passed, I talked to them less and less. This past year I'd only seen them at Christmas, and even then, I barely finished dinner before they hinted that it was late and I probably had things to do. I doubt they liked the reminder that unlike my physiotherapist sister in Toronto, I was never going to be a child they could be proud of. Never mind that Dad's biker friends saw me at the different clubs they frequented all the time. Those girls were supposed to be *other people's* children. Not his. I'm sure all I ever did was make it harder for him to enjoy himself at whichever club he ensured I wouldn't be at. I haven't even called them to tell them I'm moving. I doubt they'd answer the phone anyways.

The ride is relaxing. Music has always been my happy place, and I can just sit back on the bike with Billy Corgan in my ears and watch the prairies fly by. We stop halfway for lunch and so I could have a smoke, but we make it up to his place in record time.

He wasn't lying, his apartment is close to the college. It's a newer building with an elevator and garage parking, already way nicer than anywhere I've lived before. I'm nervous before we even get upstairs. What are his roommate and his girlfriend going to think, Tavish moving a virtual stranger in the day before he leaves? I don't know much about his roommate, only that he's a friend and military, although I guess from a different unit. There is so much I didn't understand about how all that works, but Tavish had said that while Jason was going to Afghanistan at the same time as him, he was heading there in a tank. That sounded exciting to me and somehow safer, but when I said that Tavish just snickered. I get the feeling the differences in their jobs means a lot of teasing between the two of them. According to Tavish, Jason's girlfriend, Marissa, had been spending most of her time at the apartment lately, so she'd agreed to move in just a month or so before. I guess the plan was at the end of the deployment, the two of them would look for another place together, but until then it looks like she and I better get along since we'll both be in the apartment until I find a place of my own.

My own place... every time I bring it up, Tavish changes the subject, but he must know I can't just live at his place forever. What about when he gets back? There is no way I'll find a job where I could afford the rent at this place, especially not while I'm in school, that's for sure. This all happened so fast I haven't even looked at the rentals here, but I'm sure it wouldn't be too hard to find a cheap place with a roommate or two close to the college. I'm good at finding crappy places to live. I don't want to bother Tavish too long. As much as he makes it seem like it'd be easy to just crawl under his wing and stay, that's not how life works. I don't want to give him time to get sick of me; I don't want to lose him that way.

When we get into his apartment, I'm a little shocked. It's nothing like I was expecting and suddenly I'm terribly embarrassed that he saw my place. It's spotless, with an open eat-in kitchen connected to the living area with hardwood floors and leather couches. The only thing that doesn't surprise me is the big ass

TV—all guys are predictable that way. The place isn't huge, but bigger than any place I've lived in on my own before, and even has French doors to a small balcony and barbecue off the kitchen. He takes me straight down the hall to his room, first on the right. The room looks a little more like I was expecting his bachelor pad to, with his bed on just a basic frame, some bed-in-a-bag comforter and sheets and a dresser in front with a smaller TV mounted on the wall. It also looks like the Army threw up in here. There's green boxes and bags everywhere. Most look like they're all packed to go, but there's one bag with tan and green camouflage hanging out all over the bed.

"Sorry, Jules, I hadn't quite finished packing. I thought I'd have more time and, you know, I didn't know I'd be bringing you home when I left. It'll all be gone by morning."

Suddenly, I was very sure that I didn't want it gone. Ever. The idea that he's going to disappear tomorrow has been one I've been trying hard not to think about, but that was much easier when we were in Calgary and he was in jeans. I've never even seen him in uniform. All this stuff makes it seem way too real.

He throws his backpack on the bed and looks at me. "I'm sorry I'm not going to be around to really settle you in, but this is my place. I have a TV in here, and if you plug your laptop in there, you'll have internet for email and stuff. I know you have your phone, but there is a home phone here in the kitchen, so I'll let you know the number. You can use that if you need to call long distance or whatever. Jason and I share the utilities, phone, internet and cable, and it all comes right out of our accounts, so don't worry about that part. I don't know much about the busses, but the keys to my truck are on the dresser if you ever need it. I decided to just leave it here in my parking spot. My bike was supposed to be picked up by Harley this week for storage. I guess if you're here it'd help me out if you could give them the keys and stuff. Silas and Beth will pick me up in the morning to take me to base. Oh, and there's Gunner." He points to a little bowl on the windowsill with a colourful fish inside, "I know he'll miss me terribly, so try to be nice to him."

My head is spinning now. I'm here and he's really leaving. I don't have any idea what I'm going to do next, but thankfully I don't have to think of anything because suddenly there are voices in the hall.

"All right, Cleary, let's see her."

It takes me a second to realize that "Cleary" is Tavish. Tavish rolls his eyes and pulls me back out to the kitchen where I step right into possibly the biggest man I've ever seen. I know I'm short, but this guy must be a good foot and a half taller than I am. He dwarfs even Tavish, and it's like bumping into a brick wall. I take a couple steps back to look up and see him. He has a completely shaved head and dark skin that makes his smile that much whiter. The wall just laughs as I stare up at him, and he sticks out a very big hand.

"Hey! I'm Jason Simons. I hear somehow Cleary here has roped you into hanging out here while we're gone. It's nice to meet you." His eyes move briefly down from mine and I see anger flash in them before I realize he must have noticed the bruise on my cheek and split in my lip. I wonder what Tavish has told him. I flush and look away, embarrassed, but he only falters a moment before he continues. "I'm glad to know Marissa won't be here all on her own." I realize there's a person behind the mountain in front of me when she steps out and smiles at me. She's cute, with strawberry blond curls with dark streaks cut short around her face. She's quite a bit taller than I am but still only comes up to his chest. She's curvy, with jeans and a big baggy sweater on top. It's clear she hasn't really left the house today. Her eyes are red and puffy, and I immediately feel like an intruder, but she just keeps smiling while she shakes my hand and we exchange hellos.

"I hear that Cleary is leaving tomorrow, sorry about that, you'll get used to the Army eventually. Or not… I'm headed out now so I don't have much time to say hi. Marissa's going to stay with her sister after she drops me off, but she'll be back tomorrow after work." It's not until then that I realize he's wearing a tan uniform, and his bags, just like the ones in Tavish's room, are stacked by the front door. My breath catches in my throat, but Marissa interrupts my thoughts.

"It's okay, I'm sorry I don't have more time to show you around, but I think I'll be seeing a lot of you in the next while. We can chat tomorrow, okay?" I don't understand how lightly these people are all taking this, like this kind of thing happens every day. Except I guess maybe it kind of does, for someone. This is just the first time it's happening to me.

"Oh... okay. Of course. I... um... be safe?" I have no idea what to tell someone when they're leaving for a war. Jason gives this little half smile. Tavish snickers behind me.

"He's a *tanker*, Jules. He just drives around and blows shit up. He'll probably just come back even fatter and lazier than he is right now." Now I'm staring between the two of them like they're going to fight, but Jason grins.

"Cleary is just jealous because he has to walk everywhere like a sucker. Don't worry about me, this isn't my first rodeo. I know when to duck. Looks like I'll see you when I get back!"

The two guys do their manly goodbyes; turns out they don't even know if they'll run into each other much while they're gone which seems crazy to me, but I guess that's how it works. I'm embarrassed I know so little about the military and the war. I just kind of stand there like the odd man out while Tavish grabs half of Jason's gear and the two of them head to the elevator with Marissa right behind. Suddenly, I can feel the anxiety rise in my throat and I'm stuck, heart racing and still standing in the same spot in the kitchen when he comes back in the door. He takes one look at my face, walks over and wraps me up in his arms, almost picking me up off the floor. I'm not even sure how long we stand there like that. Tavish's breaths are slow and steady, and I listen to his heartbeat against his chest, willing my body to slow down to his pace. I've done this so many times, it's like the years in between never happened. I hear his familiar voice in my ear: "Breathe, Jules. Just breathe."

Eventually, he scoops me up and carries me to his room, throwing his things off his bed with one hand then tucking me in. "I'm going to finish packing, babe. You've had a long couple of days. Just rest and when I'm done, we'll get something to eat."

I want to argue, but my body does not. I can barely keep my eyes open once I'm lying down. I watch as long as I can as he packs all that camouflage into a duffel bag. He has notepads and little gadgets I don't know the first thing about. He handles everything with total ease, like some of the pieces are an extension of him. The last thing I think right before I drift off is that this doesn't seem like just a job, and I have no idea how to love a soldier.

Twelve

Tavish

By the time I have all my kit squared away, she's completely asleep. I don't blame her, she's got to be exhausted. We've had very late nights and on top of all that, her entire world just changed. I'm surprised she stayed standing as long as she did.

She watched me for a long time without saying anything. I've been around this for years now, I forget that she has no idea what Army life looks like. What my life looks like. She's never seen me in uniform and I don't even wear my dog tags unless I'm overseas so there's really nothing about the me that she knows that would've prepared her for this. I'm suddenly curious as to what it looks like from the outside.

I step out and give a quick call to Silas. I need to head over and grab Jules' bag, so I might as well drop off my kit at the same time. He can throw it in the back of his truck and then we're ready for the early morning. I scribble a note for Juliette and haul my crap down to my truck; it's a short drive over to their place so I decide to just let her sleep.

When Silas answers the door, his face is drawn and his eyes are red. My usually carefree friend looks haggard, and I'm almost tempted to ask who we need to stomp before I see Beth standing in the background looking even worse. He's *leaving* tomorrow. So am I, I guess, but he's leaving *someone*. It's not even the same as Simons, though I bet he and Marissa had been in a similar place before Jules and I got there this afternoon. This is Silas and Beth though. They've been together so long, and even though this isn't her first time facing this, I don't imagine it gets any easier. Also, this is war. None of us were really talking about that, but that was the truth. This wasn't an exercise, it wasn't even a peacekeeping mission. It's war.

Wordlessly Silas puts on his shoes and we transfer my bags from my truck to his in the garage. I head back in through the house and walk over to Beth, giving her the strongest and gentlest hug I know how while she sniffles on my shirt. I mumble something about it being okay, won't be too long, all kinds of other things that won't help and don't mean anything. Eventually Silas follows me out to my truck.

"She's not going to be happy you saw that. She likes to think she's got this whole Army wife thing down, but the night before is always the worst. I'm telling you, Tav, having someone waiting for you at home is the best and worst thing that you can do. I won't say it's not worth it, but nights like this, man... they suck."

I just nod because I have no idea what this is like. I never really thought all the other times Silas and I have left, for one week or eight months, what it was like for Beth. What it was like for him saying goodbye and leaving her here. I realize our lives weren't really designed with a family in mind, some families just seem to work around it. I guess I knew that, but the reality of what it looks like hadn't crossed my mind. Turns out on nights like tonight, it's not pretty.

Silas heads back inside and I'm jumping in my truck when I hear Beth call my name. I look up to see her running down the driveway towards me and she grabs the open truck door, putting herself between me and my seat.

"Bring him home, Tav. I need you to bring him home safe. Please."

I kiss the top of her head as she steps out of the way and I slide into my seat, answering the only way an invincible twenty-four-year-old infantryman knows how. With absolute self-assured certainty.

"Of course."

She nods and steps back as I close the door. I look over at her one more time before driving away, her eyes drilling into me. It's that look of loss on her face that carries with me the whole way home.

What had possessed me to tell Juliette how I feel now, right before I go? I had to be the most selfish jerk. All I was offering her was that, a lifetime of those goodbyes. And that's not even including the times that I won't be able to say goodbye before I'm already out the door. She has absolutely no idea what she's getting into and I won't let her do this. I can't see her like Beth tonight. I can't make myself be the one to put that look in her eyes.

We hadn't said a single word about my confession today and I have no idea where she's at. She kissed me, but that was before. I'd thought maybe tonight there would be more, I can't deny I might have hoped for one night for us before I'm gone, but now I know there can't be. I'm not going to do that to her, not the day before I leave. Maybe never. I want her to focus on school, focus on finding herself, on starting over. I don't know what that will look like for her, but what I know for sure is she deserves more than what I saw in Beth's eyes tonight.

When I walk in the front door Juliette is sitting at the kitchen bar with the kettle boiling behind her. She startles a bit when she hears me but smiles as she looks up. I walk over and unplug the kettle.

"C'mon. I'm taking you for dinner."

She looks at me awhile before she grins. "Nope. You've given me an apartment and you're leaving tomorrow. I'm taking *you* for dinner." I don't answer, just grab the keys for my bike and pull her out the door.

We end up at a little Italian place downtown where she orders angel hair pasta and red wine and we just talk for hours, long after the bill finally comes and after we've shared tiramisu and she's had her third coffee and Kahlua. She tells me funny stories of bar patrons and I try to explain how a mechanized infantry patrol works using her lighter and the parmesan cheese shaker.

"Hmmm, it seems like those things would be easier to do in a tank. Why don't you guys just ride in tanks?" Oh, she did not.

"Jules, we are going to have serious issues if you keep making those googly faces over *tanks*." She's grinning with this mischievous smile on her face so I kick her under the table. "Not funny. I have my pride, you know. I can't have my girl comparing me to *tankers*."

Oh shit. Did I just say *my girl*? I study her face but she only briefly looks questioning before she goes back to that grin and grabs my hands over the table. "Where are we going now, soldier?" I shrug. She's never called me that before. I don't hate it.

She goes to pay the bill and I can see the moment the waitress tells her I already did that twenty minutes ago, when I told her I was headed to the bathroom. She comes back steaming mad, it's an amazing look for her. "I *told* you I was paying!"

"I'm still a man, Jules. No dice. I buy dinner."

She glares at me but I just laugh and hand her the helmet. I don't head straight back home and she's not surprised. It's our thing, it seems, to just drive until we stop. We end up at a walking path on the river valley.

"I don't know how you're not scared." she says to me as she lights a cigarette. I look at her for a moment while the flame lights her face. The shadows play on her cheekbones and I can see the damp pieces of hair stuck with sweat at her temples from the helmet. I laugh.

"Jules, I'm terrified." Her eyes get big, I don't think she was expecting me to say that. "I'm excited, sure, this is my job. I'm glad I get to go and I'm looking forward to it. I've trained for this and I'm as ready as I'll ever be. But I'm not naive, Jules. It's war and I'm scared, too. I think I'm supposed to be." I can tell she thinks about that for a minute before she answers. "It makes my fears seem silly, you know. I'm scared of going to college. Scared of trying something new, of starting over here.

Then I think, you're going to war! You're going to war and here I am, worried about finding a job or flunking my first class."

"We all have our own battles, Juliette. Mine don't make yours any less."

We're quiet for a long time as we wander through the valley. I realize after a while that we are holding hands, I'm not even sure when that happened. To be honest, I'm not sure when anything to do with Jules and me happened. Over the years, somehow, it just did. Yet here I am about to try to stop it from going any further because I can't bear to make her hurt again.

I stop walking and she turns to face me. I know she's expecting me to kiss her or to ask her to wait for me. I can't do either.

"Jules, I shouldn't have said anything to you today at the hotel. I don't want you to feel that just because you're staying at my place, just because I brought you up here... I don't want you to feel like you owe me. I don't want you to wait for me. I just want you to focus on school and making the life you want for yourself." She blinks and takes a step back, her hand goes to her pocket and she's flicking that lighter again.

"You don't want me," she says slowly, deliberately. Like she's sounding out the words so she's sure she understands.

"No, Jules, that's not what I mean at all!"

"Then what do you mean, Slick? I don't understand." She's taken another step back now and she's not looking at me anymore. I want to grab her and kiss her, dig my fingers in her hips and mark her as mine. I want to tell her that I want everything about her, I want her beside me and I want her under me. None of that, however, will change the fact that before she even wakes up tomorrow, I'm going to get on that bus and leave her here and she deserves better than that.

"Nothing has changed about how I feel about you, Jules. I'll always want you. But I'm leaving tomorrow and I can't change that. I don't want you to spend the next half year waiting for me, I want you to spend it focused on school and on finding the life you want. I've waited seven years without taking from you what you weren't ready to give me without regret, and I won't take it now right before I go. It's not fair to ask you to wait, Jules, and I need to focus when I'm gone. I need to forget about life here for six months; out there we count on each other to be one hundred percent in. I don't know if I can do that if I'm all in with you here, too. Please. When I leave tomorrow, I have to let you go."

We start walking again silently until we find ourselves back at my bike. We put our helmets on and start the ride back to my place without saying a word. When we walk into my apartment, we're both at a loss and I just stare at her for a moment. It takes everything in me not to just scoop her up and carry her to my room like a caveman. I settle for brushing back the hair that the helmet messed up behind her ear.

"I have to leave really early tomorrow, Silas is going to pick me up. So, I'll just grab my combats from my room and I can sleep out here, on the couch, so I don't wake you when I go." Jules doesn't even move, just stares at me.

"Could you put them on?" I look at her confused. "Your uniform. Could you put it on for me? I've never seen you wear it." Part of me wants to tell her no, that I want to keep her separate from that part of me, but I can't think of a good reason why she can't. She's going to see it one day, I guess. I head into my room and grab the tan combats from the back of the door.

"This isn't my regular uniform," I call out to her in the kitchen as I button up my shirt and hear her put the kettle back on. "When I'm at home, my uniform is green. These are just for the deployment." I even pull my dog tags out from the chest pocket and put them around my neck, tucking them under my shirt before I step out into the kitchen. Jules looks up from pouring her tea and just stares at me a minute. We stand there in the kitchen while she sips from her mug wordlessly until she eventually speaks up.

"Thank you. It seems real now. You look like a real soldier." I can't help but laugh and I step up close to her, bending down and looking her in the eyes.

"I *am* a real soldier, Jules."

She puts out her hand and runs it along my collar, tugging on the chain of my tags, pulling them out and cupping them in her hand before giving a little half smile.

"I didn't even know that this is what dog tags look like."

I straighten up slowly while she keeps tracing the lettering on my tags with her fingers. "You're thinking of American tags. Canadian ones look different, most people don't know that, especially if they've only ever seen soldiers on TV." She looks up at me wistfully.

"That's your blood type... I saw you write it on your helmet this afternoon. I didn't realize... I mean..." Her voice cracks so I fold her up in my arms and carry her over to the couch where I sit her on my lap and just hold her for as long as she'll let me. I've been doing this a lot these past couple days, picking her up and holding her. I could happily do it every day for the rest of my life. It seems like forever before she stirs. She stands and puts her hand out to me.

"Are you all ready for tomorrow? Is there anything more you need to do?"

"No, I got it all done this afternoon. In the morning, I just have to get dressed and go." She smiles.

"Come here then."

I follow her into my room where she shuts the door and walks up to me, puts her hand up to my shirt and starts to unbutton it. I cover her hand with mine. My restraint will only last so long. "Jules..."

"Shhh." She shakes my hand off. "Just let me. I won't do anything, I promise." Great, she thinks that *she'll* be the problem. I'm barely holding it together here. I will all of me to stand down and force my hands to my side as she finishes with my buttons and slides my shirt off my shoulders, letting it fall with a thud to the floor behind me. Then she slips her hands just under my waistband and I feel her nails graze the skin of my hips, leaving goose bumps all over me when she finds the edge of my undershirt and drags it up. I raise my arms and dip my head down and she pulls it off. Her fingers trace back down my chest, her short nails with the chipped black paint tracing a line that leads over my dog tags and back to my waist. My breath is ragged now, I wonder if she can feel my heart. I can't believe it's not beating out of my chest like some cartoon. If she only saw what she was doing to me, I don't even want to move my shaking hands from my sides. She grabs the Velcro of my belt and peels it open. My pants are heavy and it only takes her pulling free the top button for them to fall to my feet, leaving me standing in front of her in my socks and green boxer briefs. No amount of willpower or clever adjusting is going to make it any less obvious how badly I want her right now.

Juliette steps back and keeps her eyes on mine as she pulls her shirt over her head and shimmies out of her jeans. I take the time to step out of the pants pooled at my feet. Then she leans down right in front of me, close enough that I can feel her breath on my thigh as she picks my undershirt up off the ground. Fuck. Just the whisper of her hair over the front of my briefs is enough to make me twitch. She turns her back to me and drops her bra before pulling my shirt over her head.

"Lay with me," she says, and she pulls back the blankets on the bed. I slide in next to her on my back. She just lays there a minute, only our hands touching, before she ducks her head under my arm and rests it on my chest. I cover her head with my hand, holding it against me and she slides her other arm across my stomach. We both start to doze off when I think I hear her say something right as I fall asleep.

"You can let me go, Tavish, but that doesn't mean I have to let go of you."

As I drift off, all I can think is I never want to get out of this bed.

Thirteen

Juliette

When I woke up, he was already gone.

Fourteen

Tavish

The flight home is the worst. Usually a couple Gravol and I'm out, but I guess my mind just isn't willing to let me drift off so instead, I sit there swaying back and forth on that friggin netted seat, somewhere between nausea and exhaustion. That's when I should've been resting, I'm not going to have much time for that once we land. My head knows that but I just couldn't convince my body.

Silas didn't have to ask me to come with him but I guess I'm not surprised he did. We've done everything together since Basic, every course, every exercise. It makes sense that he'd want me here for this, too. I guess I'm grateful to know he wanted me around, but I also feel like I abandoned the guys back out there. Anything can happen, even in the couple weeks I'll be gone, and I can't let myself go to that place where I think about what might go wrong when I'm not there. Not that they need me, because they don't. The platoon can function without the two of us, I just don't know how well *we'll* do without *them*.

One thing I didn't expect about life on the front lines of a war is the boredom. There is a lot of that. We've played a lot of poker, I'm sure some guys have already gambled away all the deployment pay we may or may not earn out there. Nights can run really long. You can only tell the same jokes so many times, flip through the same dirty magazines, watch the same bootlegged movies on tiny laptop screens. They say that if you live with someone you grow to either love or hate them real quick. It's different out there, maybe it's the constant rocket attacks but I love *and* hate every single one of them.

Silas complains the loudest about the boredom. Most of us hate the feeling of sitting still and doing nothing, but he seemed to despise it most of all. And a bored Silas is a shit disturbing Silas. I've woken to dead snakes in my boots more than once and last week he trapped a beast-sized millipede just to put it in my helmet. He gun taped one of the privates to his cot last month, dragged him to the common area and threatened to leave him stuck there until the next rocket siren.

Okay... I may have helped with that one. That was pretty funny.

For the good eighty percent of our time spent sitting around losing our minds staring at the green walls of the tent or the endless sand landscape, there's another fifteen percent of our time that's exciting. After a little bit, our patrols started coming under small arms fire more and more frequently. All that training finally had a purpose and I don't know if I'll ever forget the first time I had to fire on a living target. When that happens, you're grateful for all those months and months on exercise, but we'll never tell the chain of command that when we get back. It seemed like every second day there was another IED set off by someone's vehicle, and whether it was ours, another unit's, or another country's, the loss is the same. We are all here for the same reasons and the flags on our shoulders don't change that.

Though I could do without the fried bread from the British kitchens. That's just gross.

It's the IEDs that are the worst, there's no retaliation for them. You can't fire back at them, chances are whoever placed it there did so hours or even days before. I guess as a soldier I never figured I'd risk being taken out by something I couldn't fight against.

Two days before Silas and I got on the plane home, we were on patrol. I was walking next to the LAV with a bunch of others, keeping eyes on the ridge. The radio chatter was light, Silas was driving again and he made a joke just before we left that he was going to fight for a medical pension for going colour blind after having to see the same tired-ass beige colour while ferrying people around this awful country. It had been an especially boring few days at camp that week and he was itching to see... something. Anything.

This is the Warrant's second tour in Afghanistan, he's a little more laid back than the rest of us but he'd just started to say something about it not feeling right when we began taking fire that afternoon. I'd just focused my gun on the only target I could see when the LAV seemed to just... explode. The sand and smoke kicked up, that sand makes everything completely impossible and I couldn't see a thing for a long while. I could still hear the rifles firing but I couldn't tell if any were ours. I dived, every breath coating my lungs with dust until I felt like I might drown in it. The radios were blowing up with commands but my ears were ringing, so I crawled over to a shape lying prone in the sand that I could see through the mess. He started to sit up before I got there and nodded at me that he was good to go. That was when we both looked over at the vehicle.

Eighty percent boredom, fifteen percent excitement and that other five percent? That's terror.

Back here at home though, it's crazy quiet. We'd only been gone just over three months before we started this little break. We are even here a couple days earlier then when my deployment home leave had been originally scheduled. Only Silas would've been able to convince me to come back here instead of living it up in some tropical paradise for a couple weeks. At least it's not too cold here yet.

While it hadn't really been that long, days there had really started to blend together while we were gone; eventually it just felt like we'd always been there, that I'd spent a lifetime digging sand from my teeth with a rifle strapped to my side. Landing back on home ground had been surreal. We had felt completely removed, I guess it hadn't occurred to me that we were still news in Canada. I wouldn't think that for long, though; there were already reporters waiting as we touched down. I cringed when I saw them but I knew it was right up Silas' alley; he always loved hamming it up for them. He used to joke that there were exactly two benefits to the military life; that girls love a uniform and that every once in a while, you get to look like the hero. He figured since he was getting married, he had to take advantage of the second one as much as possible. We worked well together that way and I'd smiled about it as we got ready to walk out. He certainly looked the hero coming off that plane. Keeping him in front of me had always meant I could avoid the camera flashes and this time was no different.

That first night after we arrived I loitered with him and Beth and some of his family for a while. We sat around talking until late in the night. Eventually, Beth was dead on her feet from it all and someone drove her back. In the end, it was just me and Silas and I stood talking with him longer than I should've before I fell into a half sleep for a couple hours sitting against a wall. I'm sure that's not how Beth envisioned her first night with him and I knew it was my fault. He should've been home with her in their bed instead of stuck there with me.

I know he wanted me here for this trip but for the life of me, I don't know why. Once he got to Beth, I just faded into the background. I'm a third wheel here and I'm sure she didn't want me hanging around as some kind of silent presence at their reunion. I tried to keep out of the way so his friends and family could see him without them feeling like they had to include me all the time. Thankfully, I've been busy since we arrived so I could stay out of their hair.

I haven't even talked to Jules since I got here. The last time we spoke was a couple weeks ago; she told me all about school and I promised her I'd see her as soon as I landed but now I'm here and I haven't called her. I know that she knows I'm here, Beth told me. I almost wondered if I called if she'd have made the trip down here to see me, but I'm too scared to ask. Mostly because I'm sure she would. I don't know what I'd say and I don't have a lot of time. I wish this trip looked different, I might even have convinced her like I planned to travel somewhere warm with me for a little while, but it's just not in the cards. Half of me hopes I'll see her every time a group of people come by, but the rest of me is too lost in my own head to think it's a good idea.

The first week here goes by as a blur, I'm still not really sleeping. I guess I was expecting sleep would eventually come easier, but it hasn't. Maybe it won't. Maybe it shouldn't, I'm sure the guys still out there aren't sleeping easy so, why should I? I'm with Silas every day and I doubt Beth appreciates it. Every time I see her I feel like just a shadow in the way, a lurking reason why she can't enjoy this time with him like she planned to before we deployed. I wish I could just leave for a while and let them be alone, but I just can't.

It's past midnight now and it's just the two of us again. I'm leaned up against the same wall, everyone else has gone home. I'm dead on my feet staring over at him and I feel like I've been in this room forever.

"Hey, you asshole, you've ruined her big homecoming." I finally tell him. "Not one single balloon, even though this place could use some. I know you said you were dreading the production of the wedding but I don't think all this was necessary just to avoid it. Besides, I know despite all that complaining about colours and balloons, you were happy to finally marry her. You should've done it years ago, you know that?"

I push off from the wall. "I'm not the right guy to do all this with you. I know we had to pick months ago, and you know I'd have wanted you here if it was me, too. But that was just us goofing off, it wasn't supposed to be how it worked. Not really. I can't do all this. I can't even get a decent night's sleep."

I've got to get back to the barracks and at least try to rest tonight. Tomorrow I need to be here early to help get him into his uniform for the big day. His DEUs are hanging up waiting along with his shiny new medal. If there's one day that he needs it all to look perfect, it's this one, and I don't trust anyone else to get it right.

"I don't know what to say to any of them, Silas. I can't help them say goodbye when I'm sure as hell not ready to. At least a dozen times a day, I find myself wishing I could call you and see if you'd take this tasking for me, you'd have been so much better at it. Beth will hate me by the time I head back and I don't blame her. Even if she isn't thinking it, between you and me, we know it's true. If anyone was going to drag the other one home early, it should've been me."

I walk over and absently adjust the flag that covers him before I walk to the door and shut off the light.

"Happy now? I guess it was only boring right up until it wasn't."

Fifteen

Juliette

I think I knew as soon as I heard Beth's voice on the other end of the phone just after midnight. Her and I'd grown close over the last few months, I'd spent a lot of my weekends drinking wine and helping with wedding plans. She amazed me, her ability to be so strong, the way she'd light up when she'd see that it was Silas on the phone and how she'd always keep their conversations positive, like she wanted to be sure that he always knew she was thinking of him, waiting for him. That combination of fiercely independent and yet also completely dependent on him was beautiful. She *could* live without him, she just chose not to.

It was such a difference from Marissa. Here I was thinking it would be a challenge, learning to live with someone I just met. Turns out that wouldn't be the problem. We got along the first few weeks, we'd chat over breakfast, watch the occasional movie together. But after that she started to be just a quiet presence; she was rarely home and when she was, she barely spoke. Then one day about six weeks in, I came home from work after midnight and she was gone, along with all her things. No number, no note. Just… gone. It almost broke my heart when I answered the home phone one night to Jason and I realized she hadn't told him. She just changed her cell phone number and left. Beth says it happens more than you'd think but that didn't help me forget the sound of Jason's voice when I confirmed what he suspected. She wouldn't be here when he got home.

So alone in the apartment, I'd thought it might be Tavish when my phone rang, I hadn't spoken to him in a couple weeks so it was about the time he'd normally try to check in. We had been keeping in touch, he couldn't tell me much but he seemed to like me updating him on my classes and my new job at the pub down the street. I'd started putting aside rent money in an envelope for him here; he never told me how much it was that he paid but I wanted to be able to give him at least what I could. I had a feeling it was going to be a fight to get him to accept it when he was back. He was due in a couple weeks for his home leave, miraculously he and Silas were going to be able to come back together and Beth had thrown together a beautiful wedding, just a few friends at a tiny venue in Calgary with a fuzzy white muff for her and a lot of balloons. I had some time off and Beth had even asked me to stand with her. I was weirdly looking forward to it; I'd never been in a wedding before and the idea of seeing Tavish made my heart ache. I didn't realize how much I'd miss him, especially since he'd only just reappeared back in my life, but I was desperate to hear his voice with every call and counting the days until I could be near him again.

But when I answered the phone, instead of the crackling of the satellite reception, I heard Beth's shaky voice on the line. "Juliette... oh my God... they're here. They're here and he's gone, Juliette. I don't know what to do. What am I going to do?!"

I jumped out of bed and threw on clothes, grabbing Tavish's truck keys on the way out. I hadn't driven his truck yet; it hadn't seemed right and the bus to school and walk to work was easy, but I figured this time it'd be okay. There was a strange car in the driveway when I arrived and a sober-looking soldier in a fancy uniform answered the door.

"You must be Juliette. My name is Captain Craig Symington and I'm the Assisting Officer. Padre Thorne is with Beth in the kitchen calling family. Thank you for coming. She needs all the support you can give right now."

I want to tell him that I have no idea what any of what he said means but I just walk into the kitchen. I feel completely numb as I watch Beth sitting at the table with her head in her hands and a phone to her ear, speaking softly to whoever it is she's called. Another soldier, I think the Captain said this was the Padre, has his arm around her as she speaks. After a few minutes, she hangs up and lifts her head. When her red eyes reach mine, she makes the worst noise I've ever heard, this strangled cry, and runs out into my arms. I just hold onto her, desperately willing myself to know what to do, what to say. I can't even process the reality that her friendly, laid back, smiling fiancé is gone. There are no words for this.

"Oh God, Jules, what am I supposed to do?" Both the soldiers look at me now and I feel completely helpless. I want to shout at them that I didn't even know what dog tags looked like three months ago, and I have no way to help her now. Instead, I run my hands through her hair as best I can and swallow my own sobs.

"I don't know, Beth. I don't know but whatever it is, I'll be right here with you, okay?"

We are up late into the night with the Assisting Officer. Once the phone calls come in that all of Silas' family has heard, he leaves to let the military know that they can release his name to the press. Silas' mom is coming in the morning and eventually the two of them will fly out to Trenton to meet the plane. But tonight, there's nothing more they can do and around three thirty, I finally get Beth to lay down and rest, and after assuring the soldiers I'll stay until her mother-in-law arrives, they leave for the night too.

As I walk Padre Thorne out, he turns to me at the door, "I understand you are… you're friends with Corporal Cleary?" It takes me a minute to even register that Corporal Cleary is Tavish. I just nod. I've been trying to keep my focus on Beth this whole time, willing myself not to think of Tavish.

"I thought you might want to know, he's okay. It's my understanding that he'll be escorting Corporal Jameson home." I give him a half smile and a thank you and he heads to the car with Captain Symington. As they drive away, I collapse onto the front step and pull out a smoke. This isn't how they were supposed to come home.

The next couple days pass as mostly a blur. I stay with Beth, sleeping in her room with her, helping keep her house running as people drop in and out to show support. I organize the meals in her freezer as they're dropped off by other wives and I keep the coffee on and the kettle hot for the steady stream of visitors. Silas' mom Dora arrives but she's in even worse shape than Beth is so I decide to stick around. Beth has so many decisions to make, arrangements, funeral plans. All I do is persuade her to eat once in a while, convince her to take showers and clean the place up when each group of friends leaves. At night, I tuck her into bed and we lie there while she tells me stories about her and Silas. We talk quietly, staring at the ceiling, sometimes she even reads me some of the letters he's written or tells me again about how he proposed. Before she falls asleep, she almost always cries about the fact that they'd waited so long to get married. She thought they had all the time in the world until they didn't.

I can't even imagine where she's finding it in her to get everything done that they ask, especially when it looks more and more each day like she's the one holding up Dora. When the time comes for her to leave for Trenton, it's the first time she's gotten dressed in anything but yoga pants or bothered to put makeup on. I packed her suitcase for her; she's going straight from there to Calgary for the funeral.

"I wish you were coming with me," she whimpers into my neck as we hug on her front step. "I still don't know what to do."

"You're so strong, Beth. You've got this, and I'll meet you in Calgary as soon as I can. Call me, anytime. Day or night. Okay?" She steps back and straightens herself again, wiping under her eyes. Captain Symington is waiting in the car with Dora. I stand on the step until the car drives away, then head back inside to clean and close the place up.

I have no choice but to spend the next week in school, which is actually a good distraction to keep me busy. It's mid-semester and as kind as my professors are being, there are things I need to get done before I go to Calgary for the funeral. I talk to Beth on the phone every night; the trembling in her voice has stilled a little and she seems just a little stronger every day, but I hate that she's doing this on her own. Her parents are not supportive of her and have never been, so there's no help there. She called them to let them know but they didn't even offer to visit, or even ask about the funeral. I don't know the story there but it didn't seem like she expected them to care. Silas was the one who encouraged her through university; he even moved her in with him and worked so she could finish when her scholarships ran out. She has Dora, but that woman is just a mess. She's a single mom, I guess they've been trying to track down Silas' dad but no one has heard from him in so long they didn't even know where to look. At this point with all the media attention, if he hasn't contacted anyone, it's unlikely he will. Dora had raised Silas and his brother on her own since they were toddlers and she just can't seem to accept that he's gone. His brother is married; he's coming in just for the day of the funeral from BC. Poor Beth is left as the only one holding things together.

I get as much work done as I can so I can take the week of the funeral off school, and when I let the pub I'm working at know I have a friend's funeral, they're more than willing to cover my shifts for me, too. I'd already planned for some time off for the wedding in a few weeks so adjusting that isn't too much of a stretch, thankfully. I've received a couple calls from other wives of soldiers in Silas and Tavish's platoon, ones I met at Beth's place, and one offers to drive me down the day before the service. Seeing this little community that I'm barely a part of come together has been inspiring.

I know Tavish is there with Beth and the family, there with Silas. He hasn't called me and I don't know what I'd say. I feel completely out of place, an outsider intruding on their private pain. I've heard bits and pieces of what happened, that Tavish was there. That he tried to pull Silas out of the vehicle after the explosion but it was too late. The selfish part of me wants to run to where he is and hold him, bring him home to me and refuse to let him go back. But this visit isn't about me. He's not here to see me and I'm not sure I can see him and remember that. So instead, I've thrown myself into trying to get ahead of my school work and supporting Beth's needs, everything and anything to keep my mind off him.

As I'm waiting for my ride down to Calgary, the home phone rings and I'm surprised to see Cleary as the name, though it's not Tavish's phone number and anyways, his cell phone is still here at the apartment. I answered it to the sound of Rebecca, inviting me to stay there with them when I arrive. I can hear Gramps in the background as she lets me know they've only seen Tavish briefly and he's staying in the barracks, but that they figured I'd be coming down and they didn't want me to have to stay in a hotel. I want to politely decline so I don't impose on them, but to be honest, the hotel was going to be using money I barely had to spend so after a few minutes, I agree. I let them know I'm not sure when I might arrive but they just tell me that the key is on the back porch and Tavish's old bed is already made for me.

The woman picking me up is named Megan; it turns out her husband is the officer in command over Tavish's company. I always assumed someone like that would be older, different, but she's only maybe fifteen years older than I am, her white blond hair is cut in a straight bob with soft features and friendly eyes. She's soft spoken and kind. As we drive, she helps me sort through some questions I have about how this all works for Beth. She'd assumed Tavish and I were a couple and while she gives me a quick questioning look at first when I correct her and say we are friends, she doesn't push. When we arrive at Dora's house, she stays briefly, offering condolences and making some notes on things she can help with during the service. She lets them know the names of the dignitaries that are attending and assures them both that they don't need to remember anyone's name or rank; of all days, tomorrow is one that they won't be expected to toe the line. In fact, she lets Beth know that she'll take care of all the polite thank yous that will be required on behalf of the regiment, that all Beth and Dora need to worry about is getting through it all as best they can. I can't help but admire Megan's presence; it's easy to forget her husband is still out there, that she must still have that fear for him buried deep. She's somehow able to say all the right things without coming across as patronizing or cold, and she excuses herself after an hour or so to give the family space.

Once she's gone, I sit up late with Beth as her nervous energy dies down. Dora has drunk herself to sleep and once she's in bed, Beth and I talk over the service tomorrow again and again until she feels like she has a handle on what it'll look like. It's a military service and most of the planning has been pulled off with the help of Captain Symington. Padre Thorne will officiate. There are dozens of soldiers from Tavish and Silas' regiment here for honour guard and they're expecting even more to come just to pay respects. It's an overwhelming prospect, all of it, so I can only imagine how out of control it all must feel to Beth. She's doing so well, though; she's found her peace and the longer we sit there and talk, the more she inspires me.

"You'll see Tavish tomorrow," she finally says as I tuck her in upstairs and I sit on the edge of her bed. My cab will be here soon, and it's well after midnight.

"I don't know what to say to him, Beth. He's not here to see me and I don't want to get in his way."

She's quiet for a long time and I almost get up, thinking she's finally given in to the exhaustion, but she speaks up.

"You know, Tavish never really talked about you, so when I met you before he left I was worried that he didn't know you well enough for this. I was worried he was making an impulsive decision. Except that Tavish doesn't really make impulsive decisions, so I knew there must be something more. That night after we left the pub, Silas told me that for as long as he's known Tavish, he's known about you. You know Tavish is the quiet, serious one next to my goofball fiancé, he doesn't let many people in. He and Silas though, they've done everything together for the past five years. They were inseparable, brothers in almost every sense of the word; they had a connection I envied sometimes. They had spent so much time together that even Tavish had eventually opened up. Did you know Tavish has kept a picture of you from high school in his helmet since Basic Training? Silas said it was funny, he felt like he knew you as soon as he saw you because you look like a better version of almost every girl Tavish has ever dated. He thought Tavish just had a specific type until he saw you and understood. Hell, I didn't even realize that tattoo on his arm was of a real person until I saw you at the pub that one night. For that boy, I think it's always been you."

I don't know what to say so I just sit there and listen while Beth lays under the covers, staring at the ceiling. I'd told her how things had been left between Tavish and me; she knew we weren't a couple. "Tavish saw me the night before they left. He came to drop his things off and he saw me. I was a mess, Jules. I'd been crying for hours. I asked things of him that I had no right to ask. He didn't say anything, but I think that seeing me is why he didn't want you to wait for him when he left. But, Jules? If you want to be with him, don't put it off. Don't wait until..." Her voice cracks and I lean down and kiss her forehead.

"I won't, Beth. I promise. You worry about you this week, okay? I'm here if you need anything, always. Call me in the morning as soon as you're ready for me and I'll come and help with everything."

"Thanks, Juliette. I don't know what I'd do without you."

The next morning it's barely after six when I make my way downstairs to the kitchen. Grandma and Gramps are sitting quietly in the nook drinking tea and they both look up with tired eyes when they see me. Rebecca gets up slowly and walks to the counter, pouring another cup and passing it to me as I walk in.

"Good morning." I give them both a quick kiss on the cheek.

"Good morning, beautiful. You must be exhausted. How is Beth?"

I take a sip of tea and sit, trying to think of how to respond. "She's... she's doing better than I'd be." I finally answer. Gramps sighs.

"I doubt it. It's times like these that we surprise ourselves." We sit in silence for a moment, this all seems a little surreal. I only met Tavish's grandparents right before we left, I'd talked to them on the phone a few times to give them updates, but how it had led to me sleeping here at their house and sharing an early morning tea, I don't know. It felt amazing, though. Like I had a family.

"I'm going to head over to Dora's early. Beth is already up and it's going to be a zoo with media and everything today. I promised I'd stick with her." Rebecca gives me a warm, sad smile.

"You're a good girl, Juliette. She's very fortunate to have you. We will be there as well, at the service to show our support, but we'll stay out of the way."

"Has Tavish stopped by?" I try to ask nonchalantly, as though it's not killing me that I haven't seen him.

"He did. He's the one that told us you'd be coming." Rebecca's face falls a little and Gramps puts his arm around her, his other hand covering hers on the table. It's beautiful to see his concern and care for her, almost like she's a part of him that he needs to pull back into himself.

"He's hurting, Juliette. This is a hell of a reason for him to be home, half of him is broken in that box with his friend and the other half is still at war. He might... if he's not himself, remember it's not you. They can't train them for this, he's in over his head. Go easy on him." Gramps never takes his eyes off his wife while he speaks.

I just nod and finish my tea.

When I get to Beth's, it's like Grand Central Station. Captain Symington lets me into the controlled chaos. There's men in dress uniform everywhere, a few of Silas' extended family have arrived from out of town, including his brother who just sits in his suit outside smoking, looking out at nothing. On the corner of the lawn, there's a news truck. It's completely overwhelming and I find Beth looking like a deer in headlights, talking to another uniformed soldier at the kitchen table.

As soon as she sees me, she jumps up, introducing me to a public affairs officer who is helping her give a statement for the news before the ceremony. What she's written is touching and beautiful but at the same time, I can't imagine summing up a life in a few paragraphs. How do you tell the world who Silas was in a couple dozen sentences?

I spend most of the time before the ceremony with Beth; she holds me by her side like a security blanket and I'm happy to be whatever she needs. Dora sways a little; thankfully Silas' brother seems to do his part by keeping her grounded, taking the pressure off Beth. She'd only met him a couple times; he lives in

Vancouver, but he seems nice enough if not a little detached from it all. When we arrive at the funeral home, the staff keep us mostly in the back, away from the hundreds of guests they're expecting. We sit in the family visiting room as military dignitaries shuffle in and out, offering quiet words of condolences. Every once in a while, I think I catch a glimpse of Tavish, but he's never there when the crowd parts. When it's time to start the service, Beth asks me to come up with her so she doesn't have to be alone with his family, and so I walk in as the piper plays, feeling uncomfortable as all the people watch us seated. I feel like an interloper, an outsider with no rights to be there, but Beth has a death grip on my hand so I'm not going anywhere.

I'd been listening in on most of the conversations she'd had over how this ceremony would work, so I knew what to expect. The coffin was carried in by soldiers in their dress uniforms; marching in step, they carry out their solemn job with honour, and Silas was placed on the waiting table in front of us, the casket open which is how Dora had wanted it, despite the strong suggestions that it wouldn't be for the best. The blast hadn't been pretty and he wasn't in the best shape, but Dora insisted that he be seen in his uniform one more time and so there he was. It wasn't until I could take my eyes off the casket that I first saw Tavish.

If I didn't know it was him, I don't know that I'd have recognized his face. Even though he has an obvious tan, he still manages to be pale and his eyes are sunken and red. It looks like he hasn't slept in weeks. He stares straight ahead, almost unseeing and I finally understand the phrase 'thousand-yard stare.' He's in that same uniform I saw him in the night before he left, but it looks different. It's worn, I'm sure it's been cleaned but it still looks dusty. There's a slight tremble to his hands where he's holding Silas' beret. And his hands, they're still bandaged, the parts I can see look red. Burnt. When I see him, I let out a little gasp and Beth squeezes my hand. It brings me back to reality, I need to be the one comforting her right now, not the other way around. I peel my eyes off Tavish and bring them back to the front, drawing little circles on the back of Beth's hand with my thumb to let her know I'm with her all the way on this.

The rest of the service is a blur. Silas' brother reads a eulogy that he and Dora had written. It's kind but I almost feel that it's missing the biggest part of his life. There's little mention of Beth and the past five years of his life. While Beth was listed as his next of kin for the military, I know it had seemed these past few weeks that with no wedding and no children, she was still on the outside looking in. Which was ironic because she'd be the one to feel the loss of Silas in her day-to-day life more concretely than anyone else. She shared his home, his bed, his entire life for so many years. Yet without that final step, it was almost as though she wasn't quite *family*.

Padre Thorne gives a message of love and duty and something, my mind is too distracted to really understand. Some commanding officer reads out some of his military accomplishments. I scan to my right briefly and see the other soldiers who had come down to attend all standing off to the side, their eyes red. For many, there were untouched tears on their cheeks as they stand without moving. God, soldiers crying must be one of the most heart-breaking sights. As I look at them, I remember a conversation we had at the pub before they left when I pointed out that Silas and Tavish were so different. "He's my brother," Silas had said, "and that has nothing to do with what we have in common. It has to do with the uniform we wear but even more than that. I trust him, one hundred percent. When we're away, we're what we've got." I wonder how many of these soldiers watching feel the same and I realize that while Silas seems to have been estranged from much of his biological family, there was a much bigger one mourning him here today.

Before I've really come to terms with what's happening, we start the procession out, walking by Silas slowly for a final goodbye.

I stand back as Beth and Dora walk up first. Dora makes a spectacle, wailing and throwing up her arms until Silas' brother comes to escort her the rest of the way back down the aisle. I go up then to Beth so she's not alone. When I look down at our happy-go-lucky friend, he looks nothing like himself; instead, almost like a wax replica, you know it's supposed to be him but something isn't quite right. I place my hand gently at the small of her back so she'll know I'm there and Beth looks up at me with a sad smile. "I thought I'd want to say goodbye, but looking at... well, he's not here, is he?"

I wrap my arm around her waist and she rests her head on mine. "No, Beth, that's not Silas. He's with you now." She takes a few more minutes before wiping her eyes and she fingers the chain around her neck, the one with his single dog tag. Then she looks down at me, signalling she's ready to go. I lead her to the door protectively, trying to deflect the eyes staring at us and give her this moment. She takes one look back as we step outside and I know.

She's let him go.

Sixteen

Tavish

I don't think I can let him go.

I know he's not there. Of all people I probably know it the best, I've been with his body every single day since I pulled him from the LAV. I'm the one that heard his screams from inside the vehicle as the fire from the explosion burned. I'm the one who didn't get there in time, the one who tried to pull him out of that hatch and instead pulled out a dead body too late.

I travelled with him in the helicopter and I sat at the airfield in Kandahar while a bunch of people who call themselves soldiers milled around me on their way out to eat. Did you know there's a Tim Hortons there? I should probably apologize to the Private that I hit when I threw the Ice Cap they brought me against the wall. A fucking Tim Hortons. Do these guys even know that there are people dying outside that fence?

I watched our friends carry him onto the plane on our way home. They looked as bad as I did and I couldn't look them in the eye. That was their goodbye, they were staying, they were still fighting. This was all they'd get. I'd be the one to watch his final trip home; they won't even have time to see it on a screen. I'm going home with him while they barely have time to shower after this before they're right back to where we were. I felt like I had no right to look at them, not when I've been given a privilege no one else will ever receive.

I've met his family and I've spoken to everyone in our chain of command. I've spent nights here and every single day. This morning I helped the staff as we dressed him in his DEUs and I may have snapped at them to leave us be when I pinned the campaign medal on his chest next to the others. The staff here would've done it for me; it's just that they don't know how to do it right.

Worst of all is all the time I've spent thinking of Juliette. What kind of selfish asshole thinks about a girl when he's here to bury his best friend? Even worse, when his other friends are still out getting shot at? I've done everything I can to try to keep her out of my head. Some of the time it's been easy, most nights I'm surrounded by the burning LAV and Silas' screams. My days have been filled with funeral planning and meetings with the family and I swear every single member of our rear party just 'checking in' to see how I'm doing, like I'm made of glass. I'm not going to break. Tomorrow I head back up to the base first thing before they put me on a plane back over. That's when things will make sense again, once I'm back there. I just need to make it through today.

I'd managed to avoid seeing Jules up until the service, I knew I'd have to see her now. Beth has told me to call her but I just couldn't. This isn't supposed to be about me. I need to avoid her if I'm going to give my all to my job here, to Beth, to the family, to Silas. I wasn't expecting to see her up there with Beth at the funeral but I guess I shouldn't be surprised, Silas had told me they'd been close since we left and Beth mentioned a few times that Jules had stayed with her at their place once she got the call. A part of me is proud of her for stepping up like that, most of me is just avoiding thinking anything about her at all.

I felt her gaze on me as soon as I walked into the funeral home. A few hundred mourners stared in my direction but I knew which eyes were hers. I stared straight ahead, I had to. My fucking hands shook like an idiot and it was all I could do to put one boot in front of the other. I've never felt so much like I didn't belong, everyone here is in their best and I'm in my combats. I'm supposed to be, I'm supposed to represent my unit. All I can hope is that they can't see what I really am. I'm not some brave soldier here burying a comrade. I'm just the broken friend with the shaking hands who couldn't save his life.

Once the funeral is done and the graveside service over, I stand to the side while the guests pay their respects to Beth and file out. The other guys from the regiment come up to me from time to time, bring me water and make quiet conversation as the people mill around. Tonight, there will be drinks at that same pub Silas and I went to with the girls before we left. I haven't had a drink or gone out with anyone anywhere since I got here, but I don't think I can get out of this one. I nod distractedly when one of the guys lets me know he'll pick me up back at the barracks once we've all changed. I hear them tell Beth about it; she doesn't want to impose on them all while they have their own way of saying goodbye, but they convince her to stop by for a little while and have a drink with them.

Jules stands with her like a protective mother. I catch her looking at me from time to time and it breaks my heart but I just can't walk over. I'm terrified if I hold her I won't be able to let go. I know Beth wanted me to see her but at the same time, it doesn't seem right that I get to be with her when Beth can't be with Silas. What kind of person would I be to rub that in her face? I need to keep my distance, I don't have the self-control to be near her.

When it's finally quiet and everyone has left, I jump in the van and head back to the barracks, throwing on the only civilian clothes I have with me and letting our friend drive me down to the Crown. Someone hands me a beer and about halfway through it, I try to remember the last time I ate anything. The week is a haze, I'm sure I've eaten but I don't remember what or when. I don't know if I've had anything today at all. The beer sits heavy in my stomach and I find myself with another far too soon. It looks like soldiers make up most of this place tonight and they're all sitting around drinking, sharing stories about Silas, laughing. This is how the Army says goodbye. I just still don't know if I'm ready to.

Since most of my unit is in Afghanistan, the guys here are mostly retired, from the other battalions, other units, or rear party. Many were in Bosnia with us, or served with us at some point in our careers before now. The brigade sergeant major and CO stopped in for a quick drink before politely excusing themselves so the rest of the guys could feel comfortable letting go. I imagine it'll be a long night but I don't know if my heart is in it. Tomorrow I'll head back and these guys will all still be here. I can't afford to pull out all these memories yet. Once I let them out, I'm not sure I can put them back, and keeping them locked away is the only way I'll be able to do my job back there.

Beth and Jules sit at a booth in the corner and guys go over a few at a time, chatting quietly with them. Dora and his brother even came by for a bit but he got her out of there quick. Dora won't even look at me, she hasn't since I got back here with him. She radiates hostility. Beth told me she's been drinking since she got the news and I shouldn't take it personally, but I think I should. At least she's being honest about who's really at fault here. About which one of us should really be sitting here while the other is in the ground.

It seems like everyone is coming over to me to talk about anything except what happened. They all bring me another beer, ask how the camp there is and how the rest of the guys are. Ask about the food, the missions, the bugs. They ask about the bugs but not the explosion. They want to know about the weather but not about how he died screaming while his skin burned. Well, the truth is I barely remember the heat of the days but I can't forget the fire or the sound of his voice. I keep my answers polite but I'm not making any friends tonight. I've barely heard a word anyone's said.

It's getting late when I stumble into the back hallway. This is the spot we stood when I told Si that we were leaving early. Where he told Beth. My head spins and I feel the entirety of the past couple weeks hit me at once. I just need five minutes where no one is asking me about Afghanistan, where no one is talking about Silas and everyone stops treating me like I'm a ticking time bomb. I splash my face with some water in the bathroom and run my hands through my hair while I look at myself in the mirror. I'm drunk. I should head back to my room and sleep it off for the trip tomorrow.

Except when I walk out of the bathroom, I bump right into her. She looks nervous and it pisses me off because the last thing I need is one more person who's walking on eggshells around me. When I look at her face, though, my chest squeezes. She's so beautiful. Her makeup shows the signs that she's been crying but it only makes her eyes look clearer. She's wearing a soft blouse that's far more conservative than anything I've ever seen her in, buttoned up near her collarbone with billowing sleeves to each wrist, it hides almost all her ink. She has a black skirt on that's tight but sits below her knee, the butterflies on her calf barely peek from underneath. The heels are all Juliette though, still almost dangerously high and incredibly sexy. When I finally glance at her face, I realize her look is far less nerves and far more desperate. She's all loving and compassionate and searching. What I should do is hold her, hold her and let her hold me and stay like that as long as we can. But I don't.

"Tavish." She's still looking at me and I know she's waiting for me to say anything. I have no words. She continues, probably just to fill the air between us. "I just put Beth in a cab, she's exhausted. Tomorrow I'll drive home with her."

I just nod, like this is a normal, everyday conversation and it's been less than months since we've seen each other. We stand there in silence for a little while longer and finally she looks as though she's going.

"I… I just wanted to see you. I don't want to bug you, though, I know you have a lot going on, I just wanted…"

Before she finishes, I'm on top of her, my mouth covering hers and I'm pressing her against the wall. I'm not gentle or romantic, I'm greedy and desperate. She mews softly and places her hands gingerly around my neck. What the hell am I doing?

My brain is disconnected; all I can think is that I need to feel something. Anything. I need to *feel*. I don't even register what's happening when my hand has pulled her blouse from her skirt and creeps up her skin underneath. My other hand reaches behind her and lifts her up onto my hips and I stumble a little, carrying her like that back into the bathroom. I'm amazed I have the forethought to lock the door before I set her on the sink. I unbutton her shirt, my hands desperate to touch every inch of her but I do it all without taking my mouth off hers. I think some part of me is scared to hear her voice because it knows I'll lose my resolve. After seven years, this was never how this was supposed to be, and yet I can't stop. I need her. I need her to remind me that I'm still here.

Once her shirt is open, I pull at my belt with one hand and unbutton my jeans. I don't even pull them down, just let them hang off my hips. I run my hand up her thigh and under the tight black skirt, I'd hiked it to her waist. She's so soft and I'm hit with the desire to stop, to take her to a bed where I can worship her body like I've always wanted to. I close my eyes, remembering all the times I've stared at her and wanted to hold her like this. How many fantasies for how many years involved my hands travelling up these legs? I take a breath to push all that back, and as I touch her, I let myself justify my behaviour a little by the fact that she's not wearing anything underneath the skirt. I knew she wouldn't be, she never is. I try not to think about the fact that her hands haven't left the sides of the sink. I can't think about any of this at all. If I think, I'll convince myself to stop. Instead I just slow until I feel her respond to me. She's kissing me; eventually her hands move around me and she traces her fingers on my neck and shoulders, but I can't pretend that even where I'm at, I don't know this isn't how I wanted it to be for us. Instead of thinking, I just use my hips to push her legs further apart and in one motion I bury myself inside her.

How she feels is almost more than I can take and I freeze. I have to break off our kiss to catch my breath; it feels like the whole world just stopped. Juliette's legs wrap around me, pulling me in closer and bringing me back to reality and she moves her hands, touching the side of my face. I feel her eyes looking up at me. I don't meet her gaze, I can't. Instead, I fist my hand in her hair, press her head against my chest and lose myself in her, her soft sounds coming in shaking breaths below my ear.

When my release comes, my legs almost give out and I'm left holding her against me like I'm trying to fuse her to my body. I stay perfectly still, my hand pressing her head into me. Everything is eerily silent suddenly, except for her soft breaths. The room spins around me and I don't move a single muscle for what seems like forever. I'm afraid if I let her go I might fall.

"Breathe, Slick." It's barely a whisper. I hadn't even noticed I was holding my breath.

I inhale deeply with my head still buried in her hair and let myself take her in. Then drop the hands I have holding her and I take a step back. In the mirror, I can see tear stains on my face even though I don't remember them falling, and the front of my shirt where Juliette's face was pressed against me is wet. I walk to a stall and grab her some toilet paper to clean herself up while I tuck myself in and do up my belt. She doesn't say a word, just hops off the sink and turns her back while she pulls down her skirt and buttons up her blouse.

When she turns around, I stare at her and I finally catch her eye. She must have cried before if my wet shirt is any indication, but she's not now; in fact, she's not anything. Her face is a mask and her eyes are cold. She smiles with her lips but I know she doesn't see me anymore, she just sees another one of *them.* I look away quickly and stare at my shoes. Shit. SHIT. What have I done?

I step back unsteady on my feet and as I lose my balance I slump down against the door until I'm sitting on the floor. I still stare at the ground, willing the room to stop spinning. I see Juliette's heels as she stands and looks at me for a long time before walking over and sitting next to me. I don't know how long we sat like that before someone pounded on the door behind me, the sudden noise tensing every muscle in me and I squeeze my eyes shut for a moment to calm the anxiety that threatens to jump up and find my non-existent rifle.

"Cleary! Driver's leaving, time to head back!"

"I'm coming!" My voice is whiskey rough and echoes in the small room, but I still don't move.

Juliette stands first and puts her hand out to me. I stare at it a second before I take it and stand up. I force myself to look in her eyes, force myself to take responsibility. The look on her face breaks me, I've seen it before, every single time I picked her up and swore I'd never be the cause. Instinctively, I raise my hand to cup her jaw, like I'm trying to protect her, from whom? Me? She doesn't move but her body stiffens. When I touch her, I swear there's a flash in her eyes where she sees me, really sees me, but it's gone just as fast, if it was ever there at all. "God, Jules. I'm so sorry." I choke out but she only fake smiles and shakes her head.

"It's okay. I'm happy I could help." Fuck. In fifteen minutes, I've destroyed the seven years I spent convincing her that she'd never have to be this for me. I can never fix this.

I broke my promise to Beth in the desert when I didn't bring him home alive. I've broken my promise to Juliette just for the chance to feel something. Except I can't feel and I can't be fixed. I couldn't save Juliette any more than I could save Silas.

I took from her.

I let him die.

Whoever I thought I was, thought I could be, I'm not. I'm no one's hero and there's no sense pretending I ever will be, now. It's amazing how fast it all went to hell.

Instead, I drop my hand from her cheek. "I'm sorry." I whisper to a face that I know will never again see me the same way, and I walk out so I can head back to the barracks and back to war, to the last thing I have left that makes sense.

Seventeen

Juliette

Four months after the funeral, we stand in the shadows, watching the bus pull up to bring the guys home.

Beth hadn't wanted to make anyone uncomfortable by being there. "It's their happy moment," she said, "their relief and joy; seeing me will take some of that from them." So, we didn't go inside the hall where they'd meet their loved ones. Instead, we just sat in the car in the parking lot and watched the bus pull up and the guys rush inside.

I held Beth's hand as we saw them all pile out of the bus. She'd needed to see this. We'd said goodbye to Silas months ago, and she really had let him go. She amazed me with her ability to move forward, every day. But she'd planned her life knowing he'd be gone until today, so she needed this moment. Seeing them all come home without him was the last piece she needed to make her heart understand. He wasn't getting off that bus ever again.

Not long after the funeral, a lot changed. Beth decided to stay in Edmonton, she had nothing to go 'home' to and she had a job and friends here. Thankfully, Silas had done the right paperwork and she received his benefits which made affording to continue to live in their little house a possibility for her. She still hated living alone and after a few weeks of me spending every night there, she asked if I'd move in with her.

I'd been packing up the few things I owned when the phone rang at Tavish's apartment. It was Jason. He was in Germany and, as it turned out, he was coming back early.

Well, most of him was. His left foot wouldn't be making the trip.

He just wanted to warn me, though he said he wouldn't be staying at the apartment. He'd be in the hospital for a while and after that, he'd need to find a place that had easier access, at least until he was out of the wheelchair. His parents would be coming, though, to his place. I could hear the lingering regret in his voice; he'd called back there to tell me because there was no one else there for him.

It was later that night that my phone rang again and this time it was the satellite phone delay. I hadn't talked to Tavish since the funeral, I didn't quite know what to say.

"Jules, Jason is going to be coming home." He spoke before I could think of words.

"He called. Are you okay?"

"Yes, I'm fine. Different jobs, remember? I wasn't there, I actually just heard." Now he sounded annoyed.

"Oh, right. Sorry." I muttered. I hate that I can't really read him over this crackling line. Stupid phone delay made it impossible to have a conversation. "Slick, I'm really sorry this happened again."

"I'm fine, Jules. No reason to feel sorry for me, the friends around me keep getting blown the fuck up but nothing ever happens to me. Nothing. I'm safe, I'm always *fine*." He said that last word like it was a curse instead of a blessing.

"Okay, Tavish, if you want I…"

The delay works against us and he speaks before he hears my voice, "I just called to give you a head's up. Help him out if you can, okay? With Marissa gone, he doesn't have anyone there."

"Of course, Slick. I've got this."

"Thanks. Okay, I better go and let guys with families call home. Bye." With that, he was gone.

I got the details of Jason's return and Beth and I went to see him in the hospital the first day. Beth and Jason had known each other well, it turns out, since Jason would usually stick around when they hung out at Tavish's place, and he was known to come out with them from time to time. I think to Beth, having him there meant she finally got her homecoming, as it was. She even brought balloons.

"Hey!" His booming voice called out to us cheerily when we arrived. He tried to sound happy but seeing him there in the bed, he seemed so much smaller than that first day he'd crowded me in the hallway outside Tavish's room. He smiled big at us, but it didn't quite reach his eyes. He nudged the nurse who was writing something on a chart next to him "I told you that you'd have to fight off the beautiful women who'd flock to visit me!"

For weeks, we kept up the visits. His parents had flown in so I got them a key to the apartment so they could stay there while they were in town. They couldn't stay forever, though, as much as they wanted to; they both were still working. Once they left, it was just Beth and me. His friends would filter in and out, but after a while, their visits became fewer and far between until I almost never saw them. I know Jason saw my frustration over that. One day while we ate lunch in his room at a time he usually had visitors he just quietly patted my hand and said, "They all do the same job I do, Jules. I'm just a reminder to them of what can go wrong, and they need to keep their head in the game right now."

Jason was unfailingly optimistic. I kept waiting for him to give up but he wouldn't. He threw himself into physio and every visit there was a new milestone he'd reached. Even the times when it had been one step back, he was positive; he kept telling us the more setbacks he overcame the sooner he could get them all out of the way. He was determined to walk, determined to be a soldier again. It was hard not to smile around him.

Beth was there almost every day, I think Jason became her purpose, her reason at a time she needed one. She'd stop there after work to bring dinner, sometimes even over lunch or in the mornings. So, it didn't surprise me that when he was released a couple weeks ago, she put a ramp at our front door and a bar in the bathroom and Jason moved into the main floor bedroom at our place. He needed a soft place to land and Beth needed to feel useful. Between the two of us, we could get him to appointments and make sure he wasn't alone.

With the two of them plus my school and work schedules, time seemed to get away from me, I hardly realized that the deployment was almost over. If it wasn't for that part of me that couldn't let go of the need to see Tavish again, I could've almost forgotten. My school semester ended so I'd picked up almost full time shifts at the pub over the holidays to save up for the next semester. Beth had me paying some crazy low utility bill as my part of the rent; she insisted since she didn't have a mortgage, it evened out. With my grants, I was doing well for once. For the first time ever, I have my own little car and a savings account. I was confident I would be okay and that felt good.

Beth knew they were due home when the time came. I could tell each day as it got closer, she needed to be there. So, I called Megan and asked her to keep us in the loop with the timing for their homecoming. She'd called a few days ago, and let me know when they were arriving. I reassured her that we'd keep our distance. I knew she'd welcome Beth there but I also knew Beth was right. Seeing her would make everyone's moment harder.

I'm trying my hardest as we sit here and watch to not look for Tavish. He hadn't called, I hadn't talked to him since he'd called about Jason and he hadn't told me when he'd get home. I'd assumed he didn't want me here. I don't blame him, not really. It's probably better this way, better I let him go now. I don't think going back to being just friends is in the cards for us and it's clear that whatever he might have thought before, he doesn't want more for us now.

Beth squeezes my hand right when she notices me see him. He's grabbing his things from under the bus when someone comes up and hands him something. I realize it must be his keys. I'd brought his truck here and given the keys to Megan to be sure he'd receive them, I just hated the thought of him having to take a cab.

I'd even cleaned up the apartment and brought Gunner back; he'd been living with me the last few months. I put some basics in the fridge and made up his bed. He might not have wanted me here but I still wanted him to feel like he had a reason to go home. He looks at the keys in his hand for a minute and then looks up, almost searching, before grabbing his bag and heading to the lot. He seems so much smaller than when he left.

Once the bus is empty and we see the last of the couples and families trickle back to their cars, I go to start the engine when I see Megan and who I assume is her husband walk toward us. He has one kid on his shoulders and another on his hip. He puts them down softly and says something to them to make them stay where they are before he and Megan come up to the car and Beth and I get out to greet them. The look in his eyes is haunted and he doesn't have to say a word for me to know that no matter what everyone will tell him in the next while, he'll always feel that as his commanding officer, he failed Silas and by extension, Beth.

Beth stares at him for a moment before stepping forward and embracing him. His bag falls beside him as he lifts his arms and holds her awhile, speaking in her ear. I purposely look away; whatever he's saying wasn't meant for me to hear. Megan watches with tears falling down her face and everything is very still for a moment before a child in the background giggles and Beth steps back with a smile.

"Welcome home, Major… Mark. Enjoy your family." She's not faking her honest happiness at this family's reunion and it's apparent. Megan gives us both a quick hug and he walks back out to the parking lot with them. As they're leaving, Megan looks back at us and mouths 'thank you.' Beth and I silently get back in the car and I look at her a moment before we pull out.

"That's it, isn't it, Jules? He's really not coming home."

"He already did, Beth. He's already home."

* * *

It's almost one a.m. and Beth has been asleep for hours when the phone rings. Jason is drifting off on the couch where we'd both been mindlessly staring at a rerun of Criminal Minds. He must see the look on my face as I stare at the phone because he just says, "Jules, they're home." I exhale and answer it to the familiar sounds of a noisy bar in the background.

"Hello?" It's almost a question; it must be a wrong number.

"Oh. Oh, shit. Beth? I'm so sorry." I don't recognize the voice.

"No, no, this is her roommate. Is everything okay?"

"Ya. It is, it's just... Well, Tavish is drunk on his ass and so it was just instinct..." His words hang in the air until I realize what he did.

My voice is barely a whisper, "You were calling Silas to come get him."

"I'm sorry, I..." He's obviously also drunk and I can't help but feel sorry for him.

"No, no, it's okay. Where are you? I'll come get him and take him home."

"Really? Thanks, I'd hate to put him in a cab like this the night we get back and none of us are in any shape to drive him."

Once I have the name of the bar, I hang up the phone and stare at it awhile. Jason looks at me sadly. "I'm sorry, Juliette. I wish I could get him for you... I could come with you?"

I force myself to smile at him; he doesn't need this to make him feel useless. "No, no, it's okay. I can get him, and I still have a key to his place so this way I can give that back, too."

When I pull up to the place, I take a minute to steel myself before I walk in. I've been in a lot of bars and they stopped intimidating me many years ago, but something about walking in here makes my heart race. Thankfully, it's late and not that crowded. A quick scan of the room and I see Tavish slumped over in a booth, his eyes barely open while the guys around him are drinking and laughing. I slowly make my way over and when I get to the table, one of the guys, I'm assuming the one who called me, stands.

"You Juliette?" he asks and immediately Tavish's eyes open completely and he tries to jump up but hits his legs on the table and stumbles back down.

"I am." The guy shakes my hand. His smile when he looks back and forth between Tavish and me seems like he knows a secret I don't, but the look on his face is gone almost before I notice it. He's clearly also drunk. I'm guessing they all are, but he's standing upright and holding a conversation which makes him in much better shape than Tavish.

"I'm Matt. Thanks for coming. Sorry to call but he's already lost dinner outside; he needs to go home and none of us are driving. Here, we'll get him into your car for you."

Tavish tries to stand up again, "I can get there on my own, you fuckers." He slurs before he starts to pitch forward. Matt gets a shoulder under his arm and steadies him.

"Shit. You going to be able to get him into his place?"

"Ya, I've worked at bars for years. I can get a drunk to his room. No worries."

Once Tavish is in the front seat, Matt closes the door and looks at me, "Hey, I'm sorry again for calling. I don't know what I was thinking. Or I guess I do, I just... for one second I forgot. It's easier when I forget. I think maybe I let myself think that he was just... home. Anyways, I'm rambling. Sorry about this. Just go easy on Cleary, okay?"

"Has he done this a lot?" I ask, almost scared for the answer. This wasn't a Tavish I've seen before the funeral. I don't think I'd ever seen him this drunk. Or drunk at all. He never used to like the feeling of losing control. Matt looks sheepish.

"Not... not before. Wasn't much of a drinker. But Cyprus wasn't pretty," he says, looking at the ground. Beth had told me they'd gone to some other country to unwind for a few days before they'd come home, apparently, the Army's way of helping them blow off steam before they get back to their families. Looking at

Tavish slumped over with glassy eyes through the window, I can't say I think it worked.

"It's really okay. I'll get him back to his place. The rest of you guys going to be all right?" I glance over at the few outside smoking by the door, swaying a little in the cold air.

"Oh ya, we all live in the same area, we'll take a cab together in a bit. We all just got back, and all of us just have empty rooms in the shacks. None of us are in a hurry to get back to them, you know? But we'll get there." That's possibly the saddest thing I've ever heard, and the idea that these guys all come home without the happy reunions I saw this afternoon, to quiet rooms with no one to welcome them hurts my heart. Right now, though, I'm not sure if Tavish is going to be sick again so I've gotta get him home. I lean up and give a very surprised Matt a hug, then quickly get in the car so I don't make it even more awkward. I wonder if it's the first hug he's received since he landed. By the look on his face, I think it might have been.

Once I'm buckled in, I look over at Tavish. He's closed his eyes and his breathing has slowed, so I start driving. I don't even go straight back to his place. I find myself looping around, catching glimpses of him every once in a while, lost in my own thoughts.

I hate myself for how mad I am to see him like this. How often has he done this for me? And yet I'm angry at how out of control he looks, how broken. I hate that he's not even acknowledging me. I hate that he's not the one who called me. Mostly I hate that he's supposed to be the strong one.

It's over an hour before we're back at his apartment and I sit in the lot for a long time before I get out and open his door. When he stirs, he opens his eyes and I think he sees me, but just looks away and tries to get out. He's still barely upright so I settle as much of his weight as I can on my shoulder. He's much lighter than when he left so hobbling like that we head inside. It takes us a painfully long time to get up to his place but eventually I have him in the door and I flop him onto his bed. His eyes are open now and he stares up at me as I kneel beside him.

"C'mon, Slick, need your help getting your clothes off here. They smell like puke, you don't want to sleep in them. Help me out so we can get you under the covers and you can sleep it off."

When I look in his eyes now he looks... ashamed? "You shouldn't... I can't let you do that." He shakily sits up and starts to undo his belt and I turn away. It's clear he'd rather anyone help but me.

I hear his clothes hit the floor and when I look back, he's curled up with his arms hugging his knees on his bed in his boxers. I can see his ribs through his back. I don't think I've ever seen him so thin. He's still got some of the lean muscle that he's always had, but he's smaller and I don't think there's an ounce of fat on him. I lean over and pull the blankets over him. He doesn't even flinch, he's out cold.

I should go but I don't want to leave him just yet in case he gets sick. I put on the kettle and stare at the steam rising. I'm so lost in thought that the whistle startles me when it starts up right in front of my face and I have to grab a cloth to pull it off the stove. Suddenly I hear a thud in Tavish's room and I almost throw the kettle into the sink and rush in. I find him thrashing on the floor beside his bed.

"Where's my fucking rifle!" I kneel next to him and put my hand on his back but he rears his head back at my touch, bringing his arm along with it, and the back of his elbow connects with my eye.

I fall back on my ass and I watch him as he scrambles a bit more, searching for something invisible before he settles back and I hear his breathing steady. Realizing I'm never going to get him back up on his bed, I decide it's probably safer for him down there anyways. I pull the blanket off his bed and drape it over his sleeping form. His eyes flutter for a moment.

I'm sorry, Si. I'm so, so sorry." Then he drifts back off to sleep.

Eighteen

Tavish

I wake up in the bathroom, already puking into the toilet. It takes me a minute, while I'm bringing back up whatever shit I drank last night, to realize this is *my* toilet. At home. I haven't seen this bathroom in seven months. It starts to come back to me, getting off the bus, throwing my stuff in the door and staying only long enough to change clothes before heading out to the bar. I'd been desperately trying to avoid this empty apartment. Somehow, though, I'm still waking up here.

That's when I hear the water in the sink next to me running and I almost think maybe it's Jason. No, it can't be Jason. Jason's not here, remember? Jason would be more inclined to kick me than help me in this state, anyways. Besides, he won't be doing that anytime soon either. When I finally control my stomach, I look up to see Jules kneeling next to me, her hand rubbing my back.

I just stare at her. Her hair is pulled back and there are dark circles under her eyes. It looks like she slept in those clothes. She's handing me a cloth to wipe my face but when I take it, I get a better look at her. And the swelling around her eye… oh, fuck me.

"Did I do that?" I whisper to her. First words I've spoken to her in months. Or maybe not, I'm going to assume she's the one that brought me home, at least I hope I didn't drive myself, but I don't remember. All I know is she's here and I'm guessing that I've done something terrible. I can't even meet her gaze, I'm just staring at the start of what will be a decent black eye.

"You were having a nightmare." I hear all the blood rushing past my ears and I try to get to my feet but instead, end up hunched back over the toilet dry heaving in the bowl. Jules doesn't even move. When I finally get a grip, I stand slowly this time, flush the toilet and back up against the wall.

"I *hit* you?" I swallow the bile in my throat again at the words.

"No, Slick, you didn't. You had a nightmare and fell off the bed and I came in to see what was wrong. You were looking for something, I think it was your gun... I got in your way. That's all."

"No. That's not all, Jules." I shake my head, backing away from her; she looks so small right now. "That's not all. I can't be around you, Juliette. Don't you get it? I took from you and now I hurt you. I'm just as bad as all the others. Worse. Having you around is... the last thing I need. I need you to go. I need you to go and not come back. We have to be done."

I force myself not to look at her as I brush by and into my room, closing the door behind me. I slump up against it and sit there until I hear the front door closing. I look over at my bed, my blanket is on the floor where I'm sure I woke up.

I'm also sure that the only good thing I had left to come home to just walked out the door.

***

I've just barely fallen back to sleep, still sitting up against the wall, when I hear the front door bang open. I'm up and in the hallway before my brain even wakes up all the way, and I come face to face with a very pissed off tanker. Before I can even react to his being there, I'm somehow on my ass with a bloody nose.

"What the hell, Simons?"

I look up to see him glaring over me and it's then that I notice his entire weight is on a crutch he has propped next to him. He's got pants on so I can't see the prosthetic but I know it must be there. While I was gone, I'd check every time we crossed paths with his unit to see how he was doing. It's funny, with the little communication that we did have, I still managed to hear about it when he left hospital, about him moving into Beth's place. That's how I heard that Jules was there, too. How I found out my place would be empty.

"How does it feel, Cleary?"

I take my hand from my nose and wipe the blood on my boxers. It's not broken, even though I know Jason could've broken it. He went easy on me and when my hangover-addled brain realizes why he's there, I haven't the slightest clue why he held back. I stand up in front of him.

"Hit me again." I growl in his face and brace myself but he doesn't move.

"You want to kill yourself, Cleary, you do it yourself. You don't try to make me do your dirty work as though I don't have enough lives on my conscience, and you sure as fuck don't lay a hand on Juliette."

"Did she tell you I hit her?"

"She wouldn't tell me or Beth anything, just that she hurt herself when she was dropping you off last night. I can put two and two together though, asshole. Do you even remember anything about the night, Cleary?" When I shake my head, he continues, "Matt called. He was too drunk to think before he decided he'd call Silas' place looking for him to pick you up." I suck in a breath. "Ya. That's right. Thankfully, Jules answered the phone since Beth was asleep. She agreed to go get your sorry ass instead. According to Matt, who I called this morning when Juliette came home with a black eye and wouldn't talk, he put you in her car and she drove you here and she was fine when he saw her last. He'd like to have words with you too, by the way, since I told him what state she was in when she got home. I know she spent the night here looking after you because she didn't get home until just a couple hours ago. I'd have been here faster but, you know, I'm not so quick on my *foot* right now."

I walk past him and onto the couch, resting my head in my hands. I have no idea how I've messed everything up this fast. How long have I been home? Fifteen hours? Eighteen? It's been less than twenty-four. My head is throbbing and it feels like I've eaten sawdust. I'm also still in my underwear. I hear Jason's crutches on the floor and he comes to sit across from me.

"She says... she says she found me on the ground, looking for my rifle, and when she tried to wake me up..."

"I was hoping that's what you'd say." I finally glance up and Jason is just looking over at me, I can't read his expression. "Look man, I know for me the nightmares and the panic when I wake up, those all got a little better with time. I had them from last time I was in Kandahar, too, though they were worse this time for obvious reasons. They're not gone, but they're not every time I close my eyes anymore either. I don't know how it's going to go for you, but I do know that Juliette isn't the kind of girl who just leaves because you make a mistake like that. Trust me, between her and Beth, those women do *not* leave you alone no matter what you put them through. The second time I met her was at the hospital when I couldn't even take a piss by myself and she *still* came every single day." He grins sadly. "So, my guess is you told her to go. But Cleary? *You lost your best friend.* Ya, we're not supposed to talk about it but you know what? Not talking about my leg never made it reappear, so I'm guessing that not talking about the fact that Silas' vehicle got blown the fuck up with him inside won't bring him back, either. So, it's okay that it hurts, and it's okay that it's broken you up.

"Everyone around you is going to refuse to talk about what happened, they're going to avoid talking about him at all. Instead, they're going to treat you like you're fragile, tiptoe around you and act like maybe if they don't bring it up, you'll forget about it. You're not going to get that bullshit from me, Cleary. I know that shit doesn't help. You want to talk about Silas, we can do that. You don't want to talk about him, about any of it, we can do that too. I don't have it in me to watch you self-destruct, though, so if that's the plan, I can't help you.

"Here's the thing. A woman who has barely spoken to you in months, a woman I *know* you care about, she just picked your sad, drunk ass up at the bar and took you home, then stayed all night, even after you blacked her eye, to make sure you didn't choke on your own puke and die. And then you threw her out of here as soon as you woke up. So, I might be a piss poor stand in for Silas, but I know for a fact he'd tell you to smarten the fuck up, Cleary. Juliette and Beth saved my life when I got here, and I'd do anything to protect them. From *anyone*. So, I'm sorry that this is what you're seeing your first morning home, but either you get it together and you treat her right or you cut her loose. But don't you string her along just so you can throw her away. And I better *never* see her with another mark on her body, Tav. Not one."

I let myself fall against the back of the couch with my eyes closed. I don't know what to say. I know he's right but I don't think I can fix it. Not yet, anyways. Eventually I hear him get up.

"I've got a friend from the squadron who's looking to move out of the shacks and into a place. As much as I'd love to move back in here, I don't know how long it'll be before I'm up to it, so I told him once you were back, I'd introduce you and see if that works for you two. I'm not gonna leave you hanging. I'll keep my half of rent up until you find someone. Sooner than later, I don't really like leaving you here by yourself for too long, so I'll give you a call this week, all right?"

I nod, not really listening, and he's quiet for a minute. When he speaks again, his tone has changed. "This isn't how we were supposed to come home, man, but this is what we've got. We can do this." I don't believe this. I'm whole. I might be missing *someone* but he's missing a part of *himself* and yet he's the one standing while I can't even meet his eye. He's looking at me with far more compassion than I deserve.

"And Cleary," he adds from the doorway, "you might want to look around this place, too. I'm guessing you're not the one who filled the fridge last night, but it looks like someone made sure you had what you needed for breakfast." I hear the door click behind him as he lets himself out and I slowly open my eyes and look over at the kitchen. There's even a few bananas on the counter. I walk over and open the fridge; there's milk, eggs, bread, orange juice, even a few beers. At the end of the hall, I see a basket of the laundry from my duffel bag and the clothes I wore last night folded inside. Worst of all, sitting small and almost hidden on the slate grey of the counter is a key. Juliette's key.

I grab one of the beers from the fridge. My first thought is that I just got home and I fucking deserve this. Then I look down at my boxers, now smeared with blood from my nose. In the reflection on the stainless steel of my fridge, I can see my chest and stomach, the scrapes and cuts from the explosion that had covered me are fading away. My hands are dry but no worse for wear despite the burns that just a few months ago had been bandaged up. That makes me even angrier. Silas died. Jason lost his foot. Meanwhile, I'm standing here without even a single lasting scar and I still can't get it together.

I'm sure of one thing. I do deserve this. I deserve this pathetic beer at ten a.m. in this empty apartment. But a future with Juliette? That's the last thing I deserve. I promised I'd let her go so she wouldn't worry that I wouldn't come back, but turns out the real reason I had to let her go was in case I did.

***

This whole transitioning back to real life doesn't make a lot of sense. I have a few days at work where we all go in and sign papers, basically give them a chance to check that little box that shows I'm still alive and will probably stay that way, and then I have some time off. I remember before I left I thought I'd resent those days at work, but I think I resent this time off, more. I don't know what to do with myself.

I went out with Matt and the guys a few more times. Matt is our platoon commander and he feels responsible for us, even though we are basically the same age. He worries, especially about those of us without families at home. A few drinks in every time, though, I look at him and all I see is the prone figure in the sand

and his dusty face finally looking up at me before we watched the LAV burn. His arms holding me back. Silas screaming.

Fuck me.

I just couldn't stomach the scene after a few weeks. I'd never been the type to be out at the bar every night before and as much as I wanted to lose myself, I still wasn't. I used to hate losing control and now, I couldn't seem to stop pushing for it. I remember something Jules said once, that losing control made her feel like there were no consequences. That sounds pretty fucking good these days.

I used to have balance, between those jokers and the time I spent with Silas and Beth just having dinner or playing cards or watching movies. Now it all just reminds me that this life, with them at the bar or at home by myself, that's all I have now. After a few weeks of turning down their invitations and ignoring their calls, most of the guys have stopped trying to get me out. Matt doesn't stop though, he still invites me to join them each time. I push away the part of me that wonders if maybe he needs me, too. I can't bring myself to take responsibility for anyone else when I'm barely keeping track of myself. Instead, it's almost some sick game to me, see how long before he'll give up on me too. I'd rather if everyone did, it would make it easier.

So lately it has just been me, at home, lost in bad TV and a case of Keiths. I'm a total cliché. I tried to balance that out with time at the Battalion gym, but it was a losing battle. I lost thirty pounds in six months in Kandahar eating (or not eating) mostly IMPs and with no real chance at any exercise that wasn't just walking in the heat. Since I never seem to get groceries, my steady diet of pizza, greasy Chinese food and beer means I'm well on my way to gaining that back now, though, and probably not in the way I wanted.

Mike, the roommate that Jason hooked me up with, is decent enough, but he left for spring exercise almost as soon as he moved his shit in. That is fine by me, the whole point of staying in is to avoid company. A concept that Jason does not seem to understand because he seems to always be around. I've tried to point out that he doesn't live here anymore, but that doesn't seem to matter to him.

So, it doesn't surprise me that it's Friday night, my last weekend before I head back to work, and he walks in the door without knocking with a pizza box and a handful of movies. I see him peek in the beer case sitting on the floor in the kitchen and calculate in his head how many I've had. He just grunts, I've only had a few. He plops down on the couch, throwing the pizza box on the coffee table. He hands me the movies and with a quick glance, I grab one and throw it in.

We've done this a dozen times or more now in the month I've been home. Sometimes he's even here in the mornings, though when I think about it, I have a feeling he kept tabs and knew which nights had been the roughest when I was out at the bar and he'd come to drag my sorry ass out of bed and give me something to do so I don't drown in another bottle to chase the hangover. I am always less than appreciative of his enthusiasm, though. He just shows up, day after day, in my space. He never asks me questions, never pushes me to talk like every other well-meaning visitor I've had. We usually hang out in silence, though sometimes he tells me about his physio, about how his prosthetic is fitting and when he'll get a permanent one, about his plans to get back to work. He has an uphill battle but I'm not going to tell the guy he can't be a tanker anymore. He spent a little time at a rehab facility in the US where he had the chance to meet quite a few more amputees; since then he considers his injury minor, he calls it a 'paper cut' since it's below his knee. His positive attitude is infectious, even to *my* shitty mood.

As we sit and watch a different war play across the TV screen, I don't know if it's because the weeks of silence finally get to me, or because I feel like talking, but halfway through I look over at him and I just blurt out, "You know, when we were in the field, once we were so cold. Like freeze your fucking eyeballs cold, and I was losing it; everything had gone numb and I couldn't even think. I tried to hold it together but it was one of those times that no matter how often you do it, you just can't anymore. Silas could see me falling apart, he told me that he had an extra long-underwear top, you know, so one morning he gave it to me and with it, I managed to make it the last few days. When we got on the bus to head back home, you know how hot it gets suddenly on there with everyone crammed in headed home? I looked over when he took his stuff off, he didn't have a long-underwear top on at all, just his t-shirt, and the skin under his combat shirt was blistered red. Worst part is I didn't even know what to say so I pretended I didn't notice. I washed the shirt he'd given me that weekend at home and left it on top of his locker at work. I didn't even say thank you."

I tell the whole story staring into my beer. Jason just nods when I'm done and since he doesn't say anything, for some reason I keep talking, though quieter now.

"I should've fought harder and pulled him out faster."

Jason doesn't even blink. Jamie Foxx is yelling at troops on the TV and it occurs to me that Jason's been waiting through weeks of late-night movies and morning coffees for me to say it, like he knew all along it's what I needed to get out.

"You could've, maybe. I figure, though, that deep down you know that he was dead as soon as that bomb went off. His body took awhile to catch on, but he was already gone. The way it went down, at least the last thing he'd have known was that you were doing everything you could to get to him. He literally gave you the shirt off his back, Cleary, even knowing that he'd freeze without it. You were his brother, he loved you, and he died knowing that you were there, that you'd do anything for him, and that you were going to be okay."

When he's done talking we just go back to watching Jarhead in silence and I wonder for the first time if there's a chance he's right and I really am going to be okay. I'm not sure I want to be yet.

Nineteen

Juliette

When I get in the door after school, it's the first time in forever that I don't have to head straight to work and I'm ecstatic.

It's not as bad as it sounds. I've gotten pretty used to my routine. I have school Monday to Friday and I'm loving it. Not only that but I don't suck, either. My GPA put me on the Dean's List my first semester and it will again. After barely scraping by in high school, I never realized how much easier learning is if you care about the subject.

I work three evenings a week, then all day Saturday. Sunday is my day off. It helps that for the first time in so long I feel like I have my feet under me. I enjoy school, I like my job and my home is safe. That's huge, I've never felt so *planted* before. I love living here; it's usually quiet and there are no expectations. Just friends. And a gorgeous bathtub upstairs. It might not be as nice at the one at Tavish's grandparents' place, but it's still far nicer than I've ever had before and since Beth has an en suite and Jason uses the one downstairs, this one is all mine. I don't know how much longer I'll stay, what I'll do after school or when Beth doesn't need me around anymore, but I'm not nervous for that either. I know Beth will let me be here as long as I want and the idea that I have a place that is more a home than just a room is incredibly freeing.

There's no guy. For the first time in, well, forever, I haven't been with anyone in months. It feels almost liberating. I've even stopped shaving everything every day. Who knew that was possible?! I've gained weight since I quit smoking, which bugs me but at the same time, almost makes me feel free; my body is good for more than just selling beer and I don't have to answer to anyone about it.

The only one I've been with since I moved here was Tavish and I don't regret that, even if he does. I could never regret Tavish, only that it seems like instead of fixing things between us, I made it all worse and a thousand times more complicated. I just wanted to be what he needed for once. I should've known that I never will be. He told me he loved me before he left but I think maybe I messed that all up. It's been over a month since I dropped him off the night he got back and he hasn't contacted me. I know he's had coffee with Beth a few times but never here, never where he might bump into me. It's been more than five months since the day of the funeral, well over a month since he's been home.

Beth will still be at work for another couple hours tonight, but as I make my way to the kitchen, I see Jason on the couch in front of a Sopranos rerun. I thought Beth was a little crazy when she told me he was moving in; neither of us had any idea how to take care of an amputee. Especially one that was still reintegrating from war. His parents, though, they'd been so worried and he didn't want to leave Edmonton and his unit to go back to Hamilton to live with them. Beth insisted that he come here and after a while, she convinced him. At first, we took turns taking him to appointments, helping him around the house as much as he needed. Now he's self-sufficient; he gets himself to and from his appointments and can do most things on his own. He could find his own place at this point, even move back in with Tavish, but truth is having him here was exactly what everyone needed. Between him and Beth, the two of them have had more than their share of setbacks as we've gone along but despite this year throwing everything at them, together they have shown an incredible perseverance I don't think they would've found alone. Watching two people like them overcoming these huge odds, it's been more than enough motivation for me to keep pressing forward with school and work.

Jason's physical therapy in the afternoons takes up all his strength and as much as he pretends to be superman, I know he finds this time of day when his energy is sucked dry to be the hardest. Some afternoons I don't even think he notices I'm in the house; his eyes glaze over and I'm not sure where his head goes but it's not here.

I make as much noise as I can in the kitchen without being obvious before I grab a couple beers and plop down on the couch next to him. Beth and I learned quick that surprising Jason wasn't the best idea. We do our best to announce our presence before we get too close so we don't startle him. For a big guy who's missing part of his leg, he can move awfully fast.

"Hey, girl," he drawls, looking over at me. He smiles but his eyes are clouded. I'm guessing he's taken some painkillers after PT.

"Hey, handsome." I rub his leg that's propped up next to me and he tips his head back against the back of the couch and closes his eyes, moaning. My hands rub softly from the tight muscles of his thigh down to the edge of the socks that cover his stump halfway down his calf. His dark skin and soft hair is smooth until his knee where it's smattered with pockmarks and scars that I absently trace with my fingers while I press into his tired muscles. Jason never asks for help but I know how sore he is most days and I find myself for the thousandth time both furious with Marissa and grateful she left when she did. If she couldn't handle the deployment, she never would've dealt with this. He deserves better than her anyways.

"Girl, you keep that up and I'll never get caught up with Tony here."

I give him a swat before continuing my amateur massage. It's Friday and for once I don't have to be at work. I wonder if Jason's fallen asleep when he speaks up.

"He's going to be okay. I didn't know for sure before, you know, but I'm almost positive now." I want to say I don't know what he's talking about but he'd know I was lying. I know he's been there with him a lot since he's been back, but he's never mentioned him to me before and I never asked.

Tavish.

"I don't know what to do, Jason. I wouldn't be here without him, but he doesn't want me around." Jason just nods and I hate that he's agreeing with me. I knew it was the truth, but that didn't stop me from hoping he'd tell me it wasn't.

"He doesn't. But not for the reasons you think."

"I've never been good enough for him, Jason. We've been friends since we were so young, but it was always him rescuing me. For a while I think maybe he convinced himself I was something more, but he knows I'm not the kind of girl he wants. Tavish deserves so much more than I am and after what he's been through now, he doesn't need to be worrying about me."

Jason just stares at me for a second before letting out a slow breath. "Jules, I don't know what went on with you and Tavish before. I don't need to, I can figure out that you've been in some shitty places, but right now I see a college student who works her ass off between school and work, who gives more to her friends than anyone I've known, who is smart and funny and, you know, pretty cute for a tiny little thing." He winks at me and ruffles my hair. "So, you've got it wrong, Jules. You're more than enough. If he was always rescuing you, don't you think maybe that's why he doesn't want you around? Keeping you away is the best way he knows how to rescue you from himself."

"I don't understand, Jason. I want to be close to him, not kept away! I know he misses Silas and I want to be there for him now that he's home…"

"That's where you're missing it, Jules. He's not home yet."

Jason's eyes are closed still and I watch for a good long while as he slowly drifts to sleep. He amazes me, his optimism and drive are inspiring. Even while he sleeps, he seems larger than life; his big frame takes up twice as much room on the couch as I do. There's about as much black stubble on the top of his head as there is on his face. I used to wonder why he bothered keeping his head and face shaved when he's not working but I guess habits die hard. He has joked with us when he first got home that his prosthetic would make it hard for him to blend in. Which was funny only because he was already a six-foot-five, two-hundred-fifty-pound black man. Standing out in the Canadian Forces wasn't something he needed help doing. I didn't know him before this but Beth says he's always been like this, always smiling, confident, strong. I know, though, that underneath he's hurting. Beth won't say anything but I know she's been watching his pain pills. He's been worried about Tavish, sometimes I think a lot of that concern comes from a worry that after all of this, losing Tavish might be what would finally break him.

I'm not as strong as he is. I *know* losing Tavish would break me.

Jason's breathing evens out and I throw a blanket over the two of us and snuggle up against his shoulder as the show changes and now I'm watching Gibbs bring Abby a Slurpee. Ever since I saw the look on Tavish's face in the bar bathroom, I've promised myself that I'd make a change. That I'd be different. I couldn't handle that look, the same one I've seen on so many others, that says they're disgusted in what they've done. *Who* they've done. To see that look on Tavish, it changed everything. I've been that girl my whole life, I don't want to be her anymore.

I've proved to myself that I'm more than I thought I was. I can handle school, I can even do well. I can work without selling myself. Most importantly, I can live without a guy. I can hold myself up without being someone else's and I'll face what's coming next on my own and I'll be just fine.

It's just that, for Tavish, I don't want to.

***

Mid-week at work is slow. I love this pub and not only because I can wear an entire shirt and jeans to waitress. It's just tucked into the back of our neighbourhood, a dozen or so booths line the wall, a handful of high-top tables separating the front door from the bar. At the entrance is an old-style British phone booth and the brass from the pipes decorating the space behind the bartender gleam every time someone opens the door and the light from the parking lot shines in. It's upbeat here, the music is soft and the regulars are more interested in the sports on the screen or the company they're with than trying to cop a feel. I smile more here, not because I'm being told to earn more tips, but it's a genuinely happy place.

When I come back out from changing a keg in the back, Jeremy, our bartender grabs my arm.

"Booth at the far corner, they asked for you specifically. Let me know if they give you any trouble." Jeremy is a little protective; a good twenty years older than me, I'm sure he has kids close to my age. He has his head shaved for reasons that I'm assuming involve disguising a hairline that was already heading in that direction, a hard set to his jaw and steel blue eyes. His face is lightly marked with chicken pox scars, his shoulders are wide and his heavy-set frame looms most nights behind the bar in a long-sleeved black shirt that clings to his chest and shoulders, jeans, dark tattoos covering every inch of visible skin below his neck. Most people would find his look intimidating, which is the opposite of what your average bartender works with, but Jeremy has a smile that seems able to convince people he's still friendly enough to serve their drinks despite the gruff look.

"Will do, Jer." I'm curious, because I don't know many people, really. I've been quiet, I keep my head down at school mostly because college culture just isn't something I'm ready for, and Beth is working. If it is one of the regulars, Jeremy would know. When I get to the table, I'm no less confused.

"Matt, right? How did you know I was here?" Matt stands up when I arrive, it seems awkward, since I'm not going to be sitting down, but I think it's just a habit for him so he just gives me a quick hug before he sits again. I stand there a little shocked, but he's got a big grin on his face. There's someone with him, another soldier I'm guessing.

"I didn't. I mean, Tavish told us you worked here but I didn't know for sure you'd be here tonight. This is Twiz... I mean Rob." He smirks at the other soldier sitting across from him who stands briefly to shake my hand. He's darker than Matt, his features sharp and hard. His hair seems like it's long for a military cut, but it's shaved on the sides. His eyes are a dark brown and he looks away quickly when I meet them. "Either, or is fine with me." I just laugh, I want to ask but I figure it's more of a second meeting kind of story.

"Okay then, Twiz, nice to meet you. Can I get you two something?" They both order a beer and I head back to the bar.

"So? What's the deal?" Jeremy wipes down the counter and I don't think he's taken his eyes off me.

"It's okay, *Dad*, they're soldiers who work with a… well, with a friend of mine. I need two Stellas." I hate that I stumble on the word friend. I've really messed things up with Tavish.

"You have a friend in the infantry?" He looks at me suspiciously and I toss a napkin at him.

"Yes, I do. One of my roommates is a soldier too. I'm not a complete hermit, I know people! Those two were with my friend in Afghanistan; they just got home last month. And… wait. How did you know what they do?" Jeremy is just quiet while he pours the beer.

"Do me a favour? They're drinking on the house tonight, okay? Don't say anything until they're done, just let them know it's been covered when they ask." He smiles up at me and rolls up a sleeve. The tattoo on his arm looks like the same symbol Tavish has on his chest. Come to think of it, it's the same symbol on the jacket Matt has on, that must be how he knew. "When I got back from Afghanistan in 2002, I'd already been in for twenty years. I decided I was done after that, I was tired. Never considered how much I'd miss it when I was out." He hands me the two beers with a sad smile; the more time I spend with people like them, the more I realize that I don't think there's such a thing as ex-soldiers. "If you want to take your break, Juliette, I can watch the other table back there. It's plenty quiet, take your time."

I walk back over to Matt and Rob. I don't know why they came so I'm not sure they want me to sit down with them or anything. I figure I'll just see when I drop off the beer. "You guys need anything else? I'm heading on my break…"

"Oh, good, can you sit with us then? Promise we don't bite!" Matt moves over a bit so I can sit down. He's smaller than Tavish and his sandy blond hair has tiny tight curls on top. His eyes are soft, though, a light blue that seems even more muted by the tired look to them. He looks friendlier, more approachable than most of the soldiers I've met so far, with an easy smile and gentle words. He's taken his jacket off and as I sit, I notice a jagged red scar running from under his t-shirt sleeve down the back of his arm. He catches my eye when I notice it and absently tugs the bottom of his sleeve. I feel my face redden a little and make a mental note to keep my eyes above his shoulders.

"So, there's a few of us heading out tomorrow getting a tattoo downtown, and then we're going to head to The Ranch. I thought, maybe, if you're not working..."

I look at him a little shocked. Is he asking me out? It's not the first request I've had since I've lived here, but I've just had no interest. It's not that I don't know why, it's more that I'm not prepared to admit it. Either way, I wasn't expecting it to come from Tavish's friend. Then again, he probably never told them they couldn't, why would he? When I don't say anything for a minute, he chuckles, a dimple appearing on his cheek. He reminds me of what you would picture as the perfect guy to take home to the parents, the hometown hero, the college all-star. That is, if you look past his eyes, and his scars. Too bad that was never my type.

"I probably should've worded that better. The look on your face right now isn't helping my self-confidence since you're an awfully pretty girl and I'd like to think the idea of me asking you out isn't as bad as that reaction, but I'm hoping it's because you're just as hung up on Tavish as he is with you."

It's not until I find myself closing my mouth that I realize I was staring at him with it open. I still can't think of anything to say, though.

"Can I tell you a story?" Matt adjusts in the booth, pulling his knee up on the bench so he's facing me. I just nod.

"We all heard about you. Tav had this picture in his helmet, like a lot of the guys, but those guys are all married or close to it. Silas told us once he's had that picture for the whole time he's been in. Tav's not a big talker, you know that, but he always referred to you there as the girl he was going back to. The one he'd finally win over." I feel a sting in my eyes and I blink hard, trying to keep my face neutral but I have a feeling it'd be hard to hide anything from Matt. If he notices, though, he doesn't say anything, just continues.

"When we came under attack that one day, I was standing right next to him when we were blown back. Tavish crawled towards me but once he saw that I was okay and the LAV that Silas was driving wasn't, he ran. I don't even know how he stood up, the concussion from the blast was still ringing *so loud*. The rest of us were still trying to get our shit together by the time I saw Tav pulling himself up, trying to get to the hatch where Si was."

Matt is quiet for a while now, he's not looking at me anymore, but staring into his beer. I look over at Twiz, but he's doing the same. It's a strange feeling, knowing that I may be able to see them but they can't see me right now.

"Once I got up where he was… Jules, you have to understand, Tav was on fire! His combats were smouldering. His hands were blistering. He was trying to get to Silas, we could hear him screaming, but he was going to kill himself. I had no choice, Jules." I don't understand what he's saying, but I don't want to interrupt him. He's a million miles away. He lets out a slow breath before he continues.

"I had to hold Tav back. Physically, I pulled him down and held him there. He had to wait until it was possible for him to get to Silas without killing himself and when it was… well when it was, Silas was gone. It was my call to save Tavish at the expense of trying to save Silas."

At this, Twiz interrupts, his voice firm. "It wouldn't have mattered, and you know it. We couldn't have saved him."

Matt's eyes are red and he finally looks up at me. He looks like a condemned man, though I get the feeling the only one condemning him is himself. "I know," he whispers, but he doesn't know.

Not at all.

"Matt…"

"It's okay." He runs his hand roughly over his face and into his hair for a minute, then looks back to me. "I've never told anyone that. Not out loud. I mean, the guys were there, or they read it in the report, or they heard from others. People *know*, but I've never said it. You know, they say if you get things out you'll feel better but I'm starting to think that's terrible advice. That sucked." He smiles shyly and I put my hand on the knee that he has propped up on the bench in front of me.

"Why now? Why are you telling me?" My voice is a dry whisper.

"Because, Juliette, I know he cares about you, and I know that the way he's acting now, that's not him. I couldn't think of another way to explain why. So, it was probably the wrong thing to do, but I'm not good at this. I was just hoping… I mean, if you'd come out with us, see him…"

"Matt, he's made it clear he doesn't want me around." In my head, I hear Jason's words, telling me that Tavish thought he was rescuing me from himself.

"He doesn't know what he wants!" I think he surprises himself with his outburst and he takes a minute before he continues, his voice calmer.

"I'm not going to force you or anything, Juliette; you have no reason to trust me when I just met you. I have this feeling, though, that you might be what he needs, so I thought maybe…"

We sit there in silence for a while. I pick at the bar apron on my lap while Matt and Twiz stare off into their beer. It's obvious that it took a lot for these guys to come here. I'm completely amazed that he's been willing to share that with me just to try to help Tavish. I don't think I knew what that kind of relationship, the kind where you're willing to give some of yourself just on the chance it'll help piece together someone else, looked like until I moved here. After a while, I stand.

"Okay. Let me grab you another drink and I'll write down my number. Give me a call and let me know when you'll be at The Ranch and I'll come by. Maybe Jason or Beth will want to come with me."

They seem happy with that and eventually they make their way home after thanking Jeremy for their drinks. He tried to tell them it was paid anonymously, but the tattoo along with his obvious excitement over having a few minutes to talk Army with them gave him away. Jeremy might have paid their tab but I think they gave him more.

I wonder if I'll ever understand all of this.

****

The next night I find myself staring in the mirror in the front entrance, waiting for Jason. Beth didn't want to come, she says she has a headache but I just don't think she's up to seeing them all. I hate leaving her, but she's got a tub of ice cream and a handful of movies to watch; she assures us she's going to enjoy her time alone without Jason and me always checking in on her. Jason reluctantly said he'd come, mostly at Beth's insistence, and I'm glad for the company.

I put on some hip-hugger jeans and a t-shirt. There was a time that my bar clothes involved less than half this much fabric, but I'm not that girl anymore and it occurs to me that just kind of happened somewhere along the way this year without me trying. I'm heavier. I know I am and it still bugs the part of me that doesn't know how else to put a value on myself. When Jason comes out of his room and sees me tugging on the waist of my pants, he puts his hand over mine and kisses my cheek.

"You look great, Jules. Stop."

We planned to get there early, soon after the boys were to arrive, but I was late getting home from school and Jason was still napping from physio. Matt called when they were headed there from the tattoo shop, but that was hours ago. When we walk into the crowded Friday night bar, it takes awhile to find them in a corner. The biggest hint is the number of girls circling the area, dressed for the club and clearly ready to find themselves a good time. I can't blame them, the group of them sitting there *look* like a good time. I feel a little pang of jealousy knowing Tavish is likely on their list of possible conquests and there's nothing I can say about that.

I see Matt first and his eyes go wide before I see him catch Jason's attention. I barely see what flashes between them before Jason leads me to the bar, mumbling something about grabbing a drink first. He's almost blocked my view before I catch Tavish at the booth behind Matt. It's hard to make him out because there's a blond standing in front of him, pressed up between his knees with her hands on the wall behind his head. I freeze and stare like an idiot while his hand brushes the exposed skin on her side between her tiny skirt and top while she's talking into his ear. I see one finger slip just under the fabric as her lips brush his face and she laughs at something he says, her chest pressed in front of him. My feet won't move but Jason tugs me away towards the bar. Just as I turn, Tavish's eyes catch mine and turn to ice.

"Jason... I need to go. I'm sorry." I try to run for the door but Jason's huge hand is clamped on my arm.

"Jules. Wait. We came all the way here, let's grab a drink."

Jason keeps me boxed in against a bar stool while he gets the bartender's attention and orders me a vodka cranberry with his beer. I melt down onto the seat.

He said he couldn't be with me and I'd foolishly let myself hold on to this idea that it meant he didn't want to be with anyone right now. But that wasn't it. He doesn't want space, he just doesn't want me. I should've known. I saw the way he looked at me after that night in the pub. After seven years, he realized what kind of girl I was and he didn't want any part of that. Not for anything more than what he got. That's why I have to make a clean break now.

"Jason, I know I have no claim on him but I don't think I can watch this. I need to go."

Before he can respond, I hear a commotion behind us. When I turn to look, Matt has Tavish up against the wall, the girl from his lap earlier skittering away. Matt's eyes are fierce but Tavish's just look resigned. Bitter. Tavish is a whole lot bigger than Matt and while I'm sure the smaller man can hold his own, it's clear that Tavish isn't putting up a fight. They hold like that, with Matt's forearm across Tavish's collarbone, a fist full of his shirt, both men's hands clenched as they stare at each other. It's less than a minute, though before the bouncers are there. There's some heated conversation before Tav and Matt agree to leave so the others can stay. I just watch, dumbstruck, sipping on my drink like it's the most exciting thing in the room. After a minute, Jason grabs my arm again and tugs.

"I need to go check on Tavish, Jules, and I'm not leaving you in here alone. C'mon."

I follow behind, a little in a daze. I want to make my feet stop. I want to just go home, but I don't seem to have the energy to fight him. When we get to the parking lot, I can already hear Matt and Tavish.

"Why would you fucking invite her here? Why are you even talking to her? I swear to God if you touched her..." That's Tavish, and I want to crawl under a rock. Jason just squeezes my arm.

"Hell, Tav, of course I didn't! I invited her because she's important to you. Because I thought you might want to see her. Because I found the fucking gun, Tavish!" Matt screams the final words at Tavish, his trembling hand pointing in his face, and then it's silent. It's like even the passing cars knew to keep quiet and there's even a lull in the bass pounding from the club. The only thing I hear is my breath that seems unnaturally loud and ragged. I'm almost convinced everyone can hear it. Several moments go by before I hear him speak again, this time quieter. "Last week, when I picked you up for work. I went back up, you know, to grab my phone from your counter, and I looked around. One of the guys said you've been asking around about gun shops in the area and so I checked, and I saw it in your room. I don't care if you want a gun, Tavish, I have one. Hell, most of us probably do. Except you've never had a gun outside work before. And I saw the notes. Who keeps envelopes like that in the drawer with their gun? There was one with my name, fucker! I can't do it again... What is it for, Tavish?" His voice cracks on the last sentence and this time it's Jason I feel tense up beside me. I grab his hand and squeeze.

Tavish rakes his hands over his face and into his hair, letting himself slide down the wall of the bus shelter he's leaning against until he's sitting on the ground. "I wasn't going to... Fuck. I don't know." It's barely a whisper. Matt just stands in front of him; from this angle, it looks like his eyes are closed.

"It was my call, Tavish, to stop you from getting to him. I did it so we wouldn't lose you both, because we would have. I know you don't blame me, but it'd be okay, you know, if you did, if you wanted to believe there was a chance to save him if I'd have let you go right away. I could take that. Then, maybe, you wouldn't blame yourself. And I'd rather you hated me than this, Tavish, because if we lose you, then all my choice did was kill you both." The silence of the parking lot, with only the muted sounds from the bar behind us, is deafening. Matt's hands are clasped behind his neck like he's holding his head on, his shoulders heaving with each breath. They are quiet for so long. I look over at Jason but his eyes are closed, his face tilted up and he looks almost like he's in prayer. I hope he is. Right now, we could all use it.

"I miss him," Tavish chokes. It's taking everything in me not to run to him, but I stay where I am with Jason, my hand holding onto his like a lifeline while Matt sits next to Tavish.

"I know, man. Me too."

"I was supposed to come home and convince her to let me take care of her forever, you know? Si, he kept telling me that I needed to just do it, that it wasn't worth waiting like he did. I even bought a ring in Dubai. But I can't ask her to be with me now. She deserves someone who can take care of her and fuck, Matt, I can't even take care of myself." Tavish stares intently at a cigarette butt on the ground, like it might answer him. My head is spinning. He bought me a ring? That was before, though. Before the pub. Before he really saw me.

"That why you're trying to hurt her? Is that why you grabbed that girl as soon as you saw her come in? Don't give me some bullshit, Tavish; you haven't even touched another girl since we've been home." Matt looks up and catches my eye. I'm horrified that we are caught listening in but he holds his gaze and keeps talking, softer this time. "You think maybe you could let her decide if you're worth it, instead of deciding for her?"

I look over at the man who has carried me more times than I can count, sitting, broken on the filthy ground outside this bar. His elbows are on his knees and his head in his hands, fingers speared in his short hair. My heart is an almost painful staccato in my throat. In my head, every time Tavish picked me up somewhere flashes in front of me. Every night he rode me around on his bike until the sun came up. Every midnight coffee at Denny's. All those times he carried me, cared for me. The fact that every time, without fail, he had a helmet and pants in his bag, waiting for me. How many times he rode in a t-shirt while his jacket covered my shoulders.

I see him sitting in front of me at the abandoned building by the highway, telling me he's leaving. I see him standing up for me to Scott. I see his face when he found out I was accepted to college. The way he looked at me in the hotel room when he said he loved me.

These past four months I was putting myself together, I thought I was doing it just for me. It was for me, I know who I am now. Maybe, though, I knew deep down it wasn't only for me. Maybe I knew that I'd need to be the one standing now.

"I've already decided." I'm right in front of him now. I don't even remember walking over. I put out my hand to him when he looks up at me, his red-rimmed eyes wide and questioning.

"Hey, Slick. I'm going to give you a ride home."

Twenty

Tavish

She looks like an angel in jeans. One I certainly don't deserve.

"Jules, I…" I stumble up off the ground, my legs half asleep from the cold cement.

"Shut up." My feet are barely under me before her lips are on mine. She tastes perfect, like the vodka cranberry I'm sure she had at the bar and the gum she probably chewed the life out of on the way over. I want all of her, I want to turn us around and push her against this wall and make her mine right now, but thankfully the part of me that needs to do this right wins out. I move both my hands to her face because I don't trust them on her body. I cup her jaw and angle her up to me, running my tongue over her lips until she lets me in.

It's Jason and Matt that finally break us apart.

"So…" They both fake cough. "Simons… figure they're good… Want to see if they'll let me back in for a beer?" Matt asks and Jason snickers.

"I know these bouncers, they're too smart to let *you* in. I'll put in a good word for you, but only if you're buying!" They saunter off towards the entrance, Jason calling back, "I'll find my own ride. Don't wait up!"

I look down at Juliette smiling up at me. Her hair is falling from a bun on the top of her head, the tendrils framing her face in the hazy light from the parking lot flood lamps that glows around her. I have to keep swallowing, it feels like my heart is trying to force its way up my throat.

"Jules..." I'm stuck. My brain has short circuited and I can't remember why we can't do this. Thankfully, she grabs my hand and leads me to her little car down the street. She laughs when I come around to her side. I'm not drunk but I can't drive, either. That doesn't mean I'm not going to open the door for her. Some habits are hard to break and to be honest, this is one I'd rather keep.

I realize we're heading to my place, which is at least empty right now. She parks out front and we make our way inside. It occurs to me as we walk up that the last time she was here she carried me up and the guilt weighs on me again. Before I can give it too much thought, though, we get up to my place, she shuts the door behind us and we just stand there, looking at each other. Even in just a t-shirt and jeans she's stunning; her curves press the fabric in all the right places and even just the dip of her neck and the lines of her collarbone make my body react to her. I close the gap between us, running my fingers through the hair next to her ear. I can feel my jeans tighten as I watch her pulse speed up at her temple; everything screams for her, but if I do get another chance, it can't be like last time.

"Jules, I don't even know what to say."

"Slick. It's okay. I know I'm not the forever girl that you deserve. But let me be this for you, right now. I can do this. I *want* to do this. It doesn't have to mean anything."

Her words are like a cold shower. I bring both my hands so they're cupping her face and tipping it up, forcing her to look in my eyes.

"Yes. Yes, it does, Juliette. The only way that we are doing this is if it means something. It means everything to me."

Jules looks back to at me and her eyes shine. "Don't get my hopes up," she chokes, her voice catching. "I thought maybe, after the hotel... But I know I can't be..."

My hands holding her face shake. I did this. All I ever wanted was to show her she could be more; instead, I've convinced her I see her as less. I can't even form the right words to say before she goes on, her voice barely a whisper, if I wasn't inches from her face I wouldn't hear her at all. "I saw the way you looked at me after the funeral. I was fine to be friends with, but when it came time for the rest... Slick. I made it so long where you might have thought I was more but I screwed up. It took me a long time and a lot of mistakes to realize that you're everything for me, and I shouldn't have let you leave without telling you. It just seemed like such a dream. That someone like you would want me. I never even thought... I'm sorry that I can't be everything for you the way you are for me, but maybe you'll let me be this."

The weight of her words is almost painfully heavy as it comes to rest in my heart. My own words aren't coming, so I decide to go another route. I kneel and scoop one arm around her knees and one around her back, picking her up and carrying her to my room. I have a brief thought of how happy I am that I just cleaned the sheets and opened a window yesterday, cringing when I think of the disgusting mess it had become since I'd been home. I lay Jules down on the bed, her upper body propped up slightly by the pillows against the headboard, and crawl over her. I'd intended to just sit next to her but as soon as she's lying there, I just need to be on her. I need to touch all of her at once, to cover her, to protect her. I need her under me. I want to be all she sees. I straddle my knees on either side of her, using one hand on the headboard behind her head and the other to tip her chin up to me. I force myself to look in her eyes, even if I'm terrified of what I'll see.

Her eyes are red, the soft brown swimming in unshed tears. My chest seizes, I feel like I just ran laps and I'm breathing far heavier than I should be. I'm at an all or nothing. There won't be any going back, I can't walk away, I can't pretend this didn't happen.

She sees me. Her eyes are hurt, guarded, broken, but she sees me and that's more than I could've hoped. More than I deserve. It's all I can do to swallow that part of me that just wants to cover her like this forever.

"Jules. I've messed up with you. Over and over. I thought I was there for you when we were younger but I was chicken shit. I might have picked you up when you fell but I shouldn't have let you get knocked down in the first place. This whole time I've wanted more than I should and I kept trying and then running away when I was scared it'd cost us too much. I brought you here to Edmonton selfishly because I needed you and I told you not to wait even when that was all I wanted. Then instead of treasuring you when you were there for me still, I took from you and I hurt you. I pushed you away because I can't handle you seeing me like this, I don't want to hurt you again and I'm scared I'll never be right, I don't know how.

"Mostly, it's all messed up because I promised you friendship and I fell in love instead. The truth is, I was already falling when I promised."

Jules swallows hard and blinks up at me. "You... Still?"

"Always."

"I thought... I mean, after you came home, after we were... The look on your face, I thought it meant that you saw me the same as all the rest. I thought maybe that you realized I really am used up. I'm not enough for you, Tavish." Her voice is strangled, soft and she keeps trying to hide her eyes from me but I won't let her look away.

"Juliette, you did nothing wrong. That was me, taking from you what you weren't ready to give me. Or maybe you were, but not like that. I was drunk and fucked up, just trying to feel *something*, which is no excuse for using you to do it. You'll never, *never,* be just one of those girls to me. And I'll do everything I can to prove your worth to you."

"Tav, I don't know if I can be the girl you think I can be." A tear finally breaks from Juliette's eye, just one, and falls down the side of her face into her ear. I move my hand up her jaw and scoop the moisture with my thumb. I look down at my chest that's hovering just above Juliette's, not even touching her, which is strange because it feels like it's being crushed.

"You can't *try* to be the girl I love, Jules. I'm not in love with who you can be, or who you want to be, or who you pretend to be. I was in love with who you were seven years ago, that girl who I'd pick up at two a.m., who'd smile and laugh with me until the sunrise. I'm in love with you, this strong, independent student and friend who has grown so much this year, and I can't wait to know her more. And twenty years from this exact moment, it'll be more than I deserve if I'm looking at my wife and the mother of my children and I'll love the you that is there, too. There's nothing you can do to be the woman I'm in love with, you're already her.

"If anything, I'm terrified that I won't find my way back, Juliette, to be the man you need me to be. I keep trying and trying but I can't find my way home. Don't you see, Jules? I want to be here for you, but I'm not here at all, not really."

I'm sure now there are tears on my face. I swipe a frustrated hand over them and will the rest back. Part of me wants her to see, needs her to see what this is. What I am. She's always deserved a white knight, but I can't be her fairy tale anymore. Maybe I never could've been.

I shift my weight to one side until I fall back, turning so my back is against the headboard and I'm sitting up next to her, close enough that we are pressed together from the side, not willing to give up the contact. "I need you to know that you're perfect. You're absolutely perfect and none of this is your fault. I'm just broken, Jules."

She puts her hand on my knee. We're both still just staring straight ahead, I can see our reflection in the TV mounted on the wall in front of us. "Tav, you're going to be okay..."

"Maybe I don't want to be!" The loud bark of my reply seems to make the silence that stretches after even quieter. I look at her reflection, expecting to see fear at my outburst but I see only compassion. "There are a million ways it could've been different. I could've driven that time, I mean, Si complained every single time. I could've just driven. I could've got up faster, ran faster. I wasn't hurt, you know, not really, so why did it take me so long to get there? Worst of all, Jules, is that Matt wants me to blame him for holding me back but the truth is... well, it hurt so much, my hands were on fire and I couldn't breathe. I'm bigger, stronger. I could've fought him, fought harder to keep trying but I didn't. I was… I was *relieved,* because I'm a fucking pussy and it hurt. Don't you get it? I was *relieved* he pulled me off! I don't deserve to be here when I didn't even fight to get to him, not really, not hard enough.

"And now, Jules, now I'm here and he's not. My burns are gone. Gone! There's no sign, no reminder on my skin, nothing marks my body. I can just go on with my life like it never happened. Except I can't." My voice cracks, it's like the desperation is bubbling at the surface of my words and I don't even pretend not to cry now. I've never told anyone this. I guess she'll really see how weak I am at this point. Her thumb still traces little circles on my thigh and I let myself relax under her touch. I whisper, "And if I can't keep going like before, I don't know how to keep going at all."

For so long we are both quiet. It's surreal, thinking back to that first night we met, that this is where we'd end up. Sitting next to each other on this bed, lost in our own thoughts.

How could she possibly be with me now, knowing what I did? I'm a coward and I don't deserve her. It seems like hours before I hear her voice. She's right beside me but it sounds like she's miles away.

"When I was fourteen, Taylor Marshall convinced me to be his girlfriend. He was sixteen and he made me feel so beautiful; he even told me he loved me. He was my first everything. I figured I was too young to even think about sex but he always wanted more. After a few months of him pushing me further and further, he found out about a house party at my friend Kourtney's house; her parents were out so everyone went to her place. He'd been planning to get me to sleep with him for weeks, saying all the right things, convincing me that it was okay because we were *forever.* How naive was that, to believe forever at that age? Maybe I always knew… The party was the perfect chance. It didn't hurt as much as I thought it would, it was just awkward. As soon as it was done, he just smirked. He pulled out of me and pulled up his shorts and he was out the door before I even had my shirt back on, high fiving all his friends. Turns out they all knew what he'd planned. He never talked to me again after that; he'd just laugh when he saw me in the halls."

Her hand stills on my knee so I cover it with my own. I've never wanted to hurt anyone quite as much as I want to hurt this kid she's talking about. The air in the room feels thick and the sound of our breath fills the space.

"After that, I could've held my head up. I could've ignored all the whispers and the rumours and been something else, started over. Instead, know what I did? I gave in, because it was easier. A few weeks later, one of the boys who had been harassing me at school boxed me in alone under the stairs, talking about how he heard I was easy and wanted some of the action. I couldn't get around him and I panicked for a minute, then I made a choice. I gave him what he wanted. I could've screamed, or ran, or even just said no, but instead, I *chose* my knees. I chose to be that girl. No one made me, I made myself. Don't you see, Slick? All those nights and I never once deserved your help."

"Jules, I meant what I said before. What you've done isn't who you are. You don't have to..." Juliette cuts me off, standing up she walks over and grabs her wallet from her purse that she'd dropped somewhere on the way in here. She comes back over and sits back next to me, turning to face me on the bed, looking me in the eyes with the most beautiful expression I've ever seen.

"I can do my very best, Tavish, to try to accept that you care about me anyways. But that means you have to remember that you found me and you put me back together first."

She opens her wallet and pulls out a crumpled napkin, the edges where it has been folded are so worn they are torn in places, and she unfolds it carefully until I see what's on the inside. It's a drawing. One I recognize, because I remember sketching it while she slept at Denny's.

"I saw this when you left it on the table at the restaurant 7 years ago. Tavish, when I looked at it I barely recognized myself in it. This girl, she's beautiful. I held onto it all this time to remind me that there was someone out there who saw this in me. Even if you didn't know it, you have always inspired me to be more. Maybe that was because I was going to need to do the same for you, now. I'm not going anywhere. I want you to believe me that I haven't been with anyone since you brought me here. I haven't wanted to. I haven't needed to. It's only been you. I've never once even let myself *consider* that I might be good enough for you, in all these years. I closed off every possibility that you might want me to save myself from being let down, to preserve the friendship I knew I didn't deserve. But if you want me, I'll spend every single day doing whatever it takes. I'll help you find your way home, if you'll let me."

I thread my fingers through her hair and pull her face up to mine so our foreheads are touching. I can feel her breath whisper against my mouth. I need her to be the one to close the gap between us this time and after only a couple seconds, she does. Her kiss is soft, unsure. After a moment, she breaks away, her lips still so close I feel them brush against me when she speaks.

"Slick. I need you. Please. Show me you need me."

My hand instantly grips harder. I'm probably pulling at her hair but she just gasps softly and opens up to me, my tongue sweeping into her mouth. Her hands are suddenly under my shirt, her fingers cold against my chest. She breaks her mouth away from mine to pull my shirt over my head and I take the moment to collect myself. I'm going to do this right.

I pull Juliette's t-shirt off her slowly, keeping my eyes on hers. Then I scoop my hand under her ass and hold her up, placing her on her back beside me. I lean over her and kiss down her neck and across her collarbone, ghosting my lips to the edge of her bra before I unsnap it and peel it off her. I need to touch every inch of her skin, taste her on my lips. This time I'll worship her body the way I should've the first time.

Juliette sits up on her elbow and uses her other hand to try to cover her middle from me but I put my hand over hers and slowly move it out of the way.

"I gained weight, Tavish..." She bites her bottom lip, sucking it into her mouth, looking away. I keep kissing down her body towards her belly button.

"Jules. You're fucking amazing. You're the most beautiful girl I've ever seen. You always have been." I continue to move my lips down her stomach until I get to the edge of her jeans and wait, looking up at her until she finally meets my eyes. I need to see her eyes while I undo the buttons, kissing my way down each inch that's exposed before I get to the end and slip them down her legs, throwing them to the side. For a long moment, I just stand there over her, the soft light from the hall making her pale skin glow against the grey sheets. I wasn't lying, no one has ever even come close to this. I've never seen her this way and I want to just pause the moment so I can replay it over and over. There's something about the soft curves of her, I swear somehow, she looks even more gorgeous now than she did before.

Crawling back up the bed over her, I start at her knees, kissing the inside of her thighs until I can feel her legs quivering under me. I keep my eyes up, watching her watch me as my lips reach her centre and she shudders, moving one hand to the back of my head as her hips lift to meet me. It takes my fingers and tongue very little time before her back arches and fingers clamp to my hair, the sound of my name on her lips is almost more than I can handle and I grind my hips into the bed under me, looking for relief. When I pull myself up over her and look down at her face, her breath is still heavy as she slowly opens her eyes.

"Slick, no one has ever… I mean… that's never happened with someone else before."

I just stare down at her, her face is flushed and I'm completely at a loss. I didn't think it had been important to me, that I'd never have a first with Jules, it's not like I could give her mine, either. I realize, though, that I'm first person she's been with that cared about her enough to make it *good* for her. I hate that she's been treated so terribly, but I can't ignore what being the first does to that very basic part of me that wants her to be mine, completely.

My legs shake as they struggle to hold me over her and I don't think I have the self-control to stop right now. I still hesitate, though, with my hand on my belt, looking in her eyes until she moves her own hands down and slips them under mine, pulling my belt loose and popping the button of my jeans. She pushes both my jeans and boxers down in one motion as far as she can reach and I shimmy the rest of the way, kicking them behind me. I grab a condom from the dresser, rolling it on with trembling hands as quickly as I can. I feel her heat against me, my body pressed against hers. I settle myself between her legs and I can't help how my hips grind against hers. She closes her eyes and moans softly but I gently tip her face with my hand.

"Look at me." I hold her eyes and trace my hand down from her chin, across her soft stomach and guide myself into her, watching her expression closely as I push inside.

"Fuck, Juliette. You were made for me." Her mouth opens in a silent cry and I move my arm above her head, putting my weight down on my elbow. I press my open lips to hers in a desperate, never-ending kiss. There are a thousand ways I've dreamed of doing this but right now, I just want to rock into her, completely and relentlessly, savouring the feel of having her perfect body under me until I can't hold back any longer. With my other hand between her legs, I gently stroke her until I feel her clench around me and I follow her release, swallowing her moans so they're only for me. Eventually, I collapse on my side next to her.

Rolling over, she just ducks her head under my arm onto my chest, cuddling up so her whole body lies flush with mine like this is the most normal thing in the world. Strangely, it feels like it is. I go to put my hand against her head to hold her to me but she grabs my arm. I'd completely forgotten about the new tattoo, now looking a little red around the edges, inked across my forearm. I should probably clean that before it scabs tonight, I know better than to treat a brand-new tattoo this roughly, but it's been a long night. I'd forgotten it was there. She gingerly traces the lines of the soldier's cross, the boots, rifle and helmet with Silas' dog tags hanging over them.

"This is beautiful, Tavish," she whispers.

I absently turn my arm over to the pin-up tattoo she knows is her on the other side.

"This arm... I thought this arm would now just be a reminder of the people I'd lost along the way. The people I was responsible for."

Juliette pulls herself up off the bed and walks to the bathroom. I take my time enjoying how comfortable she seems gloriously naked in my apartment. I hear the water running, a moment later she's back with a warm washcloth and a bottle of Lubriderm. Crossing her legs next to me on the bed, she takes my arm and softly presses the cloth to the new ink, cleaning off the sweat of the day before adding just enough of the unscented lotion to keep it from drying up too badly. When she's done, she tosses the cloth towards the laundry basket and places the lotion on the table beside the bed. Pulling the blankets up over us, she settles back down where she started, with her head on my chest.

"I'll never be able to express how sorry I am that you lost your best friend. I wish I could've known him better. But Tavish? You've never lost me. Not for one moment, not since we were teenagers, not once."

ALL THE WAY HOME

Twenty-one

Juliette

It's funny, I guess maybe I thought just being *together* would make it all better.

Four a.m. that first night, I learned that only happens in romance novels. I had all these plans in my head, a romantic breakfast, a long overdue talk. Then Tavish mumbles in his sleep and I am only half awake listening before the mumbles turn to yelling. I'm lying on my side with him wrapped around me from behind when all of a sudden, the arm around my collarbone slips up and tenses, trapping my neck and shoulder in a triangle that has me clawing at his arm like my life depends on it. He finally relaxes just a moment before I black out and I slip under his elbow, sliding down and kicking my feet back against his thighs until I push myself off the bed. I sit there then, staring at him. His eyes are even open a bit but he is still fast asleep. I can barely make out the words he is saying, mostly what sounds like military jargon and panic. I try to speak to him, try to keep my voice soft and comforting. I reach out my hand to touch him, to calm him but he twists at my intrusion, smacking my hand away in anger. Eventually he sits up, looks around fitfully and then collapses back down on the bed, his breath ragged for a very long time before it seems to drift back off to a steady rhythm. By the time I catch my breath, huddled on a corner of the bed staring at him, I can see the light seeping in from behind the curtains and I shuffle to the kitchen to make a coffee.

When he stumbles out of his room an hour or so later looking for me, I'll admit that my ego is bruised. Why isn't he comforted by me? Isn't that how this works? That he just needs me and he'll be able to sleep soundly as long as I am by his side? Shouldn't love chase away his nightmares?

"Hey, Jules... Why are you up?" His voice is strained, I can tell he's hoping that my answer will be different than the one he's expecting and I briefly considered lying, but I can't bring myself to do it.

"You... had a bad dream, I think." That's all I can say. He looks down at his feet, leaning against the corner of the kitchen wall in a pair of tight boxer shorts; he closes his eyes tightly. He's put some of the weight he lost back on, the muscles in his arms twitch as he clenches and unclenches his fists. The sharp lines of the muscles on his chest and stomach are highlighted by the soft light creeping in from the window. Even with the tortured look on his face, the sand-etched lines and the tremble in his hands, I'd still call him beautiful. Even more than he was the first time I saw him seven years ago. "You scared me, Slick."

"I'm sorry. I'm so sorry. I should've slept out here... I should've said something. Did I hurt you?" Tavish doesn't even look up. It's only been a matter of hours and already he's ashamed and I'm hurt. I don't know why I thought this would magically be easy.

"No, not at all." I instinctively rub my neck a little but there's no pain, he just scared me. "And I didn't want you to sleep out here. I wanted you to sleep with me."

I plop down on the couch and after a few long moments, he comes and sits next to me. He apologises over and over, but it isn't his fault and I just can't admit that I'm not mad at him. I'm mad at myself. After all that, I'm not enough. I'm not what he needs.

"I think... I think with time it'll get better. At least that's what Jason said. He said I just need to give it time. And next time I come back, maybe it won't be so hard. I'll know what to expect." Tavish still isn't looking at me as I'm finally grabbing my things to head to work. I'm already going to have to rush to get home and change before I head to the pub.

"What do you mean, next time?" I'm stunned.

"Juliette, this is my job. I won't be home forever. I mean, it'll probably be a year or so but I'll go back when my unit does. I won't let them go without me." I stand, frozen by the door.

I knew this, right?

I didn't know this. Not really.

"I want to do this, Slick. I just... I haven't even got you home yet. If you leave again... how many times? How many times before you never find your way back? You'll never lose me, Slick, but I don't know if I can stand here and watch you lose yourself."

Tavish opens his mouth to speak when his phone rings. He glances at it instinctively in a way that shows he has no intention of answering, but his face tightens at what he sees on the screen and he grabs it. It's still early morning and I wonder who it is for only a moment before I hear him answer.

"Gran, is everything..."

The words die on his lips and I hear the hitch in his breath before he falls into a sob.

"Please... Gramps..."

Twenty-two

Tavish

I don't even remember the drive here. As soon as I hung up the phone, everything was a blur. I don't know what I'd have done if Jules hadn't been there. I don't even know if I could've made the calls. Instead, I found myself staring at my silent phone while she was a blur around me. I must have changed into the clothes she handed me and next thing I know, she had a bag with her and we were out the door in her little car, with a five-minute stop at her place where I sat in my seat and waited while she grabbed a bag before we were headed to Calgary.

Standing on my grandparent's front step, the same step I've walked up a thousand times to the house I lived most of my childhood, I just stare at the door. My Grampa gave me everything, he's the only father I've ever known. I think maybe if I just don't walk in, I can pretend he's still sitting inside, sleeping in front of the TV with a whiskey glass next to him and Gran at her sewing machine. If I go inside, though, I'll have to see that he's not. Not since Gran found him this morning, in that exact spot but never getting up again. She told me on the phone it was 'quiet.' I've seen more death than I ever thought I would. None of it was ever 'quiet.'

Juliette's hand presses on my back as she comes up behind me and I feel myself instinctively lean gently into it. She never said a word on the drive here, I can't imagine having to spend that trip with anyone else. Our silence wasn't awkward, or forced. It was just there, like we both knew there was no need for words.

Eventually I turn the handle and step inside. Gran is there with one of her friends, sitting at the kitchen table having tea. It all seems so ridiculous to me, like they should be *doing* something. I'm not sure what I expect them to be doing. I drop my bag and walk right over to her, kneeling in front of her chair to hold her. She sniffles on my shoulder as tears fall down my face. "I'm so sorry, Gran... I'm so sorry..." I can't think of anything else to say.

"The Good Lord takes us home in His time, my Tavish. Your grandfather and I had an amazing fifty-three years together, more than I could've ever asked for." She leans back and cups my face. "He was the love of my life, and I'll miss him terribly. But he was confident in his eternity and I know he wasn't scared to make this final trip Home. I bet he's up there smirking; he always told me he'd have to go first because he couldn't live without me."

"I wish I would've..."

"Now, Tavish, no. Don't you start. Your grandfather knew you loved him and you had nothing left unsaid. Even if you thought you did, trust me, he knew. He was so proud of you, my boy."

At that, I let her hold me, still kneeling in front of her like a child, ashamed that I'm the one being comforted instead of the other way around. Minutes pass, it feels so much longer, before I hear Gran speak again.

"Juliette! Thank you from bringing Tavish here for me. Come here, sweetheart, get yourself some tea." I stand up on shaky legs and look hesitatingly at Jules, but my embarrassment is met with the most beautiful empathy I've ever seen. Something about her has always quieted my heart and even now it's no different. She comes over and hugs Gran, giving her a kiss before she turns and I wrap my arms around her. She's so much smaller than I am; from the outside, it probably always looks like I'm the one holding her, but nothing could be further from the truth.

"Thank you," I whisper into her hair and she just gives me a squeeze before she heads to grab some tea and I pull up a chair. Gran and I talk a little about all the logistics of death. If I hadn't been part of everyone going through all these plans with Silas six months ago, I never would've realized how much work is involved when someone dies. Gramps didn't want a funeral, though; he just wanted to be cremated quietly, and Gran seems content with that choice. Instead, we'll have this weekend, a house of friends and happy stories of his life. It was 'him,' as she said, he was never interested in ceremony. There's not actually much to do here, once we have it all gone over; they'd planned very well for this and Gran will be just fine. I knew Gramps would've made sure of that; he took care of her in every way it made sense he'd take care of her even now. Jules and I still decide to stay the weekend, though, so she's not alone, though she has many friends from her church who assure me they'll keep her close and I believe them. Her freezer is already almost full with meals, her cabinet full of wine, her tea pot always hot and there's always a friend in that chair when she needs one.

After long talks that lead into many, many stories and laughter as various friends drop in or call, it's getting late and eventually it's just the three of us sitting around the table with the last of the Chinese food cartons in front of us. I see Juliette start to get up to clear the table but this time I stop her. She's been going and going since this morning; it's like she fell back into the routine she found with Beth. It occurs to me what she's doing is what my mom should be doing. How bad is it that I completely forgot about my mom in all this?

"Gran? Did you call Mom?"

Gran looks at me wistfully. "Of course, I did, sweetheart, but you know your mom. She said she'd call later and see if I needed anything." I wish I was surprised, but I'm not. Instead, I'm not even disappointed. I'm more in awe that just by being herself, Juliette is a far better daughter to Gran than my mom has ever been.

Grabbing the empty foil containers of ginger beef and chow mein, I head into the kitchen. Once I have it all put away, I walk through the house, room by room, making note of all the little things I can come back to fix up. I'm going to have to step up with Gramps gone.

When I get into the living room, I see the shadow box Gran made for Gramps a few years ago, with his medals from the war. Gramps had been barely eighteen when he joined and left for

Korea; he hadn't met Gran until the year after he returned. I don't know a lot about how it all happened but from what I understand, they were married quickly but had a hard time having a child. Mom wasn't born for almost ten years, well after they'd given up hope. Gramps had finished his military career shortly after, releasing to Calgary and working at a machine shop until he retired completely when I was in high school. I often wondered if he could've retired years earlier had he not been raising me, but he'd never made me feel like a burden. I'd been given everything I needed and Gramps had been more than enough of a dad for me.

Making my way back to the kitchen, I can hear Jules and Gran talking quietly.

"I want to be what he needs, Rebecca, but I'm not. He still has nightmares, even when I'm..." Juliette trails off and my initial shock at her words is gone as I stifle a laugh when I realize she's embarrassed to admit she was in bed with me to a woman who raised her teenage daughter's child. Gran just laughs.

"Oh, Juliette, I wasn't born yesterday. Let me ask you something though, sweetheart. All those years when you were lost, could Tavish have 'fixed' you?"

"Of course, not. It wasn't his fault, I just wasn't in a good place..."

"Exactly, my dear. Love doesn't work that way, not in real life. Spence and I, we were married over fifty years. All those things that the war broke, all those bad habits he came with, I didn't fix a single one. Look at this," Gran gets up slowly and walks over to the couch where Gramps always sat, picking up an edged whiskey glass and absently swishing the little bit of water inside. "I can't bring myself to bring this glass back to the sink. Every day for fifty-three years, I've picked up this glass. Oh, I nagged him. Yelled at him. I'd get so angry every time I had to pick it up myself. Until one day I realized that I never put my boots away. I always leave them on the mat, I figure I'm going to need them again, so why would I? Spence, though, he'd come home and he'd put his boots in the closet, and then he'd put mine there, too. He liked things in their place. I asked him once if it bothered him and he just told me, 'When I see your boots, it reminds me that you're here when I get home, so I don't mind.' So, you see, my dear, some things didn't need to be fixed. This glass, it'd remind me in the mornings that he'd been home with me the night before. And now... now I can't bring myself to put it away one last time." Her voice breaks and Jules covers her mouth with her hands, her eyes shining with tears. After a moment, Gran sits back down. "Some things, you learn to let go. And some things, you work on together. Korea never left Spence, no matter how many nights I held him in our bed. You'll do well to learn that neither of you can fix the other, not on your own. It takes time and hard work, and both people have to be invested, have to work at it together. I'll tell you what, though," Gran leans forward and I barely catch her words to Jules, "the two of you have spent too much time so restless, waiting to get where you already are."

I'm still trying to figure out what she means when Jules looks up and catches my eye. I see the shock register on her face, wondering how much I've heard. I just smile, I don't even intend to but just looking at her makes me just a little happier than I am when I'm not. How's that for messed up romantic?

I help Gran up to bed and when I come back down, Jules is standing near the door. It occurs to me that she's not sure where she'll sleep. She opens her mouth and I have a feeling she might suggest a hotel so I decide to just shut it right down.

"Juliette, you've done more for my family today than I have and you'll sleep here, in my room. I can sleep on the couch, and I will if you'd like me to, no problem. I've done it many times before when guests have stayed here. But I'd really like to sleep next to you. I won't touch you, I just... I'd just rather be close to you tonight if you'll let me. I understand if you're afraid, though."

She just takes my hand and we walk upstairs. Ten minutes later, I'm curled up beside her as she listens to me tell her stories of Gramps until we both give in to sleep.

I don't want to push her. I don't want to spook her, not when she's here in my bed. I won't be the one to make the next move, she knows how I feel. She's here with me now, and I wish I knew this meant forever. No matter what, I'll take tonight.

ALL THE WAY HOME

194

Twenty-three

Juliette

I let the weeks pass without seeing him. The drive from Rebecca's after we'd said our goodbyes was almost as quiet as it had been the way there. I don't know what I wanted. I guess I needed him to ask me to stay, but he didn't and I didn't blame him. He'd given me everything and I'd almost walked out that morning. If he hadn't gotten that call, I don't know what I'd have done. I hadn't wanted to put any more strain on him over the weekend, not when he'd just lost his grandfather, but after I talked to Rebecca, I knew I had to let him know that I wasn't giving up. I wanted to tell him that I was wrong, that I cared, that I'd stay. When I'd opened my mouth to say something when I dropped him off, though, he hadn't even let me say a word.

"It's okay, Jules. It's okay, you don't have to say anything. Maybe it was just a dream, that we could be together. I don't want to lose you completely, you mean too much to me. Let's just give it time, okay, and then maybe we can go back to how things were."

After that, he'd just kissed me on the top of the head, like he always did, and walked inside.

I guess he wasn't willing to fight like I was.

School's almost out. I just have a couple exams left before summer break and I'll be working at the bar full time then. Jeremy has even scheduled me a shift or two a week working in the office with him, helping with ordering and marketing.

I could've called Tavish, I guess, to see how he was doing. He said to give it time, though, and I was thinking maybe the distance would help.

It doesn't.

Instead, it feels like all we ever have is brief moments together sandwiched between long, painful absences. Maybe that's how it's supposed to be for us. Maybe we were only intended to be the occasional comfort for each other and nothing more. The idea twists in my gut and hurts far more than I'd hoped.

He promised he loved me. He had told me that before but I foolishly let myself believe him this time. Except Rebecca was right, I walked out at the first sign of trouble, convinced myself that I couldn't 'fix' him when I was expecting it to take no effort at all. When just my presence didn't erase his pain, I gave up and hurt him. Again. How many times would I hurt him? It was best I stayed away now. Problem is, I didn't guard my heart this time. Love has never factored itself into any relationship I've ever had, but it had taken everything in me not to admit to him, admit to myself, that I'd let myself fall so hard this time. Who am I kidding? I spent years pretending that I didn't love him, it took no effort at all to let that guard down. I wanted to run back, tell him I'll fight with him, for him. I wanted to tell him we can do this together, no matter how hard it's going to be. I couldn't bring myself to do it, though. Instead, I let him go and walk around day after day pretending my heart is still in my chest.

Matt and Twiz have become regulars at the bar and tonight Jason and Beth have even stopped in. The four of them have been sitting at the high top most of the afternoon and evening, chatting lightly with each other. I'm almost always laughing when they're around, which makes the time pass quicker and I'm almost ready to close up. Every once in a while I catch myself watching the easy way Matt and Twizzy get along and I realize that this is what Tavish lost. I know he could have it again, with them. With Jason and Beth. With all of us together. I just don't think he's willing to risk it, but it hurts my heart that he's letting himself sit on the outside.

I hadn't even told Beth what happened. She knows I stayed over with Tavish that night, she knows I was in Calgary with him when Gramps died because she'd offered to come down. Tavish had told her she didn't need to; instead, they'd planned a trip for a bunch of us during summer break so the guys could do some home repair and Beth and I could visit with Rebecca.

Matt knows, too. I'd been the one to message him first about Tavish's grandpa. I know all four of them had probably expected to witness our happy ending when we returned, that they'd be watching Tavish and me walk into our future together. It must be clear, though, that's not what happened, since I haven't seen him since we got back. No one said a word, though, and I don't know if Tavish has said anything but I think they're just waiting for me to want to talk about it. So far, I just can't.

I grab their glasses to fill up when Matt looks up from the phone he was typing on over at me. "You must be happy Tav comes home today."

"Oh." I try to sound nonchalant but Matt is the one person I can never fool. Not about Tavish. I've grown to appreciate our friendship over the past little while and casual flirting aside, it might be the first time since I met Tavish that I've settled into an easy relationship with a guy who's not interested in anything else. Matt is the kind of person who's always worrying about everyone around him, trying to make sure the other guys are okay, doing far more than expected to try to make things right for them. I've found myself wondering, recently, if things are ever all right for him, but I don't think he gives himself half the attention he gives everyone around him.

I might as well just be honest with him, he can read me like a book. "I didn't actually know he was gone."

He gives me a puzzled look. "Where do you think he's been this past month? He was sent on course out of town, but their flight came in this afternoon, I sent a driver for them right as I was leaving work."

I pretend to busy myself washing the same spot on the bar for a while. I'd assumed he'd been avoiding me, that he was done chasing me down. It hadn't occurred to me that he might not have been in town. That would have to mean that none of them know how badly things broke down between the two of us. Even I can't wrap my head around how fast it all fell apart, right after it finally came together.

I've never really had the kinds of friends I confide important things to, no one who cared to listen, anyways. Looking at these four, I think right now might be the time I change that.

"I might have messed this all up, guys. I don't know that I can do this, this whole military thing. I don't understand it and I don't know how to make it better. He's a soldier, he's always going to be a soldier, and I'm not as strong as you, Beth. He's going back, you know, one day. I just don't know how to be what he needs."

Surprisingly, it's Jason that speaks up first.

"I'd been to Afghanistan before, you know that. Coming back that first time, I'm not going to lie, it was hard. I even found myself sleeping on the floor some nights; my bed just seemed wrong, almost suffocating. I was always on edge, every little thing set me off. Eventually, though, it settled down to manageable and I realized looking at everyone else around me that it was normal. That I was okay. Some guys weren't, you know; they couldn't do the job anymore, and I don't think I'll ever understand why it affects everyone differently or why I was okay when they weren't. I just know that when the time came up that I could go back, I was ready. I wanted to go. I hate the Army some days, Jules, but I love being a soldier. I went back because I wanted to, and to be honest, I'd go back tomorrow if I could. I don't know what it's like to have that one person at home that is waiting for you, I thought I did but looking back, Marissa was never going to be that person. It's not the deployment or the Army that ends relationships, those things just test them. Mine failed, but that's not the standard you should look to. The good ones, they only get stronger. It's not easy when we're always gone and we come home a little broken. Or, in my case, in a couple pieces. Everyone right here knows that there are risks that one time the damage might be irreparable, or we might not make it home at all. We all decided our job was worth that risk and we'll be lucky to find women willing to accept that."

Beth looks at Jason a long while, then back at me with a sad smile. "You don't fall in love with the uniform, or the days away, or the war. You fall in love with the person, and the rest is just part of the journey you go on together. Even though it might not seem like it, even knowing that I'm here, now, without him, I have to say that it was worth it. And you, Jules, are so much stronger than you think."

I try to let that sink in. Tavish first told me that he wanted to join the military when we were teens that first night we talked. I guess in my heart I let myself believe that losing Silas meant he'd walk away from it, but looking at these four at the bar, I realize that none of them are walking away. They're moving forward, as best they can, and they might not even always be in the military, but they'll always be soldiers. So will Tavish.

The front door of the bar opens and light pierces into the dimness, I squint my eyes as I try to see how many people have come in so I can grab menus. I only see one figure, shadowed by the brightness streaming from the outside and it's not until I get to the other side of the bar that the door closes and I see who it is.

Tavish is still in uniform, and the way he's staring at me is enough that his friends at the bar let their greetings die on their lips while I walk towards him. It's like he doesn't see another soul in the room. I open my mouth to speak but when his feet are just inches from mine, he cups my face in his hands and just when I think he might kiss me, he lets go and drops to both knees right in front of me. I think I hear Beth make some kind of squeak noise behind me.

"Juliette. I told myself I couldn't keep chasing you. That I'd wait for you to be the one, this time, to find me. I knew I was lying to myself. Just like I knew I was lying to you seven years ago, when I said I'd be your friend. Juliette, here's my confession: I knew that was a lie the moment I said it. I've loved you since I threw that helmet to you when we were seventeen years old. I need you, Jules. I've lived my life thinking if I could just be your hero, I could win you over, I could save you. Instead, I'm broken and scared and fucked up sometimes and *I'm* the one who needs *you*. This amazing person in front of me? The one who's accomplished so much this year? You did this. You didn't need me. You don't need me. But Juliette, I'm here hoping that you still want me." At that, he grabs something from his front pocket and that's when I realize I'm crying because I can barely see the small black box between my tears.

"I spent this past month trying to convince myself that I was making the right choice, to do this job, even if it means doing it without you. Now I'm here, making an ass of myself in front of you and our friends and this bar, because I realized that I can't. I'm selfish, Juliette, and I need both. I need to be a soldier, it's who I am. Except I can't do it without you. I need this job and need you to do it.

"Please, Juliette. Marry me. Let's go home together."

The pub is silent, I think Jeremy might even have turned off the music. It's more likely that I just can't hear it; all I can hear are Tavish's ragged breaths and my own heartbeat. I drop onto my own knees and I raise my hands to his face and brush my thumb on his cheekbone. All the words I could say are jumbled and all that comes out with my nod is, "I love you, Slick."

His entire face relaxes. "Are you sure?"

"In a thousand years, when the rocks are crying out and the mountains fall into the ocean that has waited since creation to be filled, I'll look back on our life together and I'll still know with perfect clarity that right here in this moment is the first time that I was absolutely sure that I'd still be in love with you then. I love who you are, the you I met eight years ago, and the you that is willing to make a fool of himself right here for me. We can't go home together, though."

His face falls. "Why? I'll do anything, Juliette…"

I shake my head slightly, running my hand down his collarbone to his arm until I grab his hand.

"Gran was right. We've been trying to take each other home for so long and missing the point. Right here, when we are together, wherever we are, Slick, we're already here."

Twenty-four

Tavish

I don't think she's ever looked so beautiful.

Sitting there in her cap and gown waiting to be called, she hasn't seen me yet. She didn't know if I'd make it, I'm in the middle of pre-deployment training, but thankfully we were in town and Matt pulled some strings. Matt, Twiz, Jason and I are still in our combats and we're drawing a few stares as we sneak in late but I barely notice. We find Beth in the back of the auditorium. Twiz and Matt are goofing off as they check out every female graduate that crosses the stage, groaning loudly about how long it's taking, but when the announcer calls out for Juliette Parsons, they're on their feet just as fast as I am and I love the look on her face as she walks across the stage to collect her diploma and she hears us hooting and hollering from our seats.

I know we're making a scene and I don't care in the least. She deserves every bit of it.

The four of us in uniform make for a fidgety bunch and I'm trying to act like a respectable member of society while I wait for the rest of the graduates to have their time but sitting still has never been my favourite skill. When it's finally over, we make a beeline out of there. My anxiety isn't what it used to be but hanging out in this crowd of people while they push their way to the exits isn't my idea of a good time, and I know the rest of the guys feel the same. Between us all, though, we probably look a little intimidating and people get out of our way quick so we are one of the first to the grounds outside as we watch the rest file out.

Any time I'm here with Jules I'm always amazed at what the world looks like from this perspective. I'm only twenty-six, these *should* be my peers. This fall I head on my third deployment, though, and I couldn't feel further removed from them.

Looking at the guys with me, I don't really mind. I have my family, such as it is. For all the worry I'd had that by asking for more from Juliette, I was taking away her only real friendship, the reality was she gained the opposite. She and Beth are closer than anyone and Jason, Matt and Twiz, well, the three of them love her just as fiercely as I do, just in an entirely different way. Watching her adjust to that kind of love, it's been beautiful to watch. Her parents aren't here today, even though Jules had been talking to them more frequently than she had before; they'd been 'unable' to make the trip. I know it hurt, especially since they'd flown to Toronto for her sister's graduation a couple years ago, but Juliette had let it roll off her back. Her accomplishments had all been her own and I think a part of her was more than happy to enjoy this victory without them.

I look up into the crowd to scan for her just as a tiny body slams into me and Juliette's legs wrap around my waist, her gown bunching at her hips and her face nuzzling into my neck. I take a quick glance at Matt—I *am* in uniform and even hand holding should technically be off limits—but he just grins. There's got to be exceptions for every rule.

"You came!" She has all the excitement of a little girl on Christmas morning; her smile is contagious as she leans back and her eyes dance as she looks at me.

"You can thank Matt for making it happen. I'll do anything to be there for you when I can, Jules. I'm so proud of you." She hops down and gives Matt a kiss on the cheek. There are few people who can get that close to her without me trying to contain the need to break their hand for touching her, but these guys have earned the exception. He just winks at her and she hugs him, Twiz, Jason and Beth before looking back at me.

As we head out, Beth and Jason walk up ahead together and she bumps her shoulder against him as they share some secret between the two of them, Jason grinning down at her. He's back in uniform, which is what he wanted, but it's been an uphill battle and I don't know how long he'll pull it off. He's still living with Beth and technically Juliette, though most of Jules' stuff has slowly ended up at my place now. I know he could've moved out by now but I doubt he'll be ready for it anytime soon. Beth's place is like a comfort blanket for him and she seems to thrive on having him there to look after.

Matt and Twiz finally moved out of the single quarters and into a condo together. While Twiz seems to have a revolving door of women in and out of his room, Matt's is noticeably quiet. For all his effort in making sure the rest of us land on our feet, I wish I could say for sure that he did. I also wish I could be to him what he is to us, but I have no idea how. Instead, we'll leave soon back to Afghanistan at the end of this summer for another half year and I hope he finds the redemption he's looking for there. He's the only one who thinks he needs it.

Juliette stops a moment when she looks back at me. "Hey… that's different." She scrunches up her face looking at my epaulet and I laugh. I love how clueless she can still be about anything military, even though she's been all but living with me this past year. "Does this mean you're not a corporal anymore?"

Matt slaps me on the back. "You're looking at Master Corporal Cleary, now. He's kind of a big deal."

Jules hugs me again, although her feet stay on the ground this time. "I don't really know what that means, but I'm so proud of you anyways. You have a new name!" Everyone laughs this time. I'm instantly nervous, though. They all know why as they look at me.

"I'm hoping, Juliette, that you'll let me change one more name this weekend."

She looks at me confused and I take a moment to appreciate everything about the way she looks. She's beautiful, and the woman she's become makes it even more so. She's learned to stand on her own and I'm so grateful she's let me stand with her while she's done it. This summer she'll start as manager at the pub and in the evenings, she's going to work on her undergrad. She can do absolutely anything and it's changed even the way she looks. Her eyes are different, clearer, filled with purpose. I love them this way, even more because I got to see them transform.

The guys can't hold back their grins as they circle around; they know what's coming but I didn't tell Beth. She doesn't like to keep secrets and anyways, it's more fun for her this way. Juliette and I hadn't talked about when we'd get married, even though she's had my ring over a year now. I spent the first while healing, Jules even convinced me to get some help and my nightmares have subsided with time. I've been able to keep on, and learned to be grateful for that instead of guilty when so many I know haven't been able to do the same. Now that I'm looking at my next deployment, though, it's time to do more than just talk about a date.

"Jules, I don't even remember a time that I didn't love you, that I didn't want more than anything to be your knight in shining armour and rescue you. Then when Silas died, I thought that meant my dream died, too, because I couldn't rescue anyone. But you, Jules, you always amaze me. It turns out, you didn't need me to save you. You came here, you made a home, you loved my friends, you worked your ass off and now, look at you! I'm so proud of you. You did this and you didn't need me to do it.

"I'm so grateful though, that as strong as you are on your own, you still want me beside you. I know this year was hard; you not only accomplished all of this, but you helped me heal. I know next year will be hard, too, when the time comes to say goodbye for a while. But when I leave, Jules, I want to go knowing that this is forever. So, I have some tickets to Vegas in my pocket and a couple wedding bands in my bag. If we leave tonight, the six of us, there's a little white chapel on the strip with our name on it tomorrow. If there's anything I can do to honour Silas, it's to take his advice and marry you now, no waiting. What do you say?"

There's tears down her cheeks, spilling onto her hand that still covers her mouth. Her diploma clatters onto the ground with her forgotten hat as she slides off my bike and into my arms. In that moment, it's never been clearer that I could be anywhere, my condo, her house, or the parking lot next to my bike.

As long as she's with me, I'm home.

Dear reader

Tavish and Juliette's story is fiction, but the realities of deployment and reintegration for military families is definitely not. If your homecoming hasn't been 100% Youtube worthy, let me assure you that you are not alone. That shit is hard. Sometimes, it's so hard you can't do it on your own.

If you feel like you're drowning, I encourage you, most of all, to reach out to the support network in front of you. Whether it's family, friends or your military community, let someone in. Finding solid ground again is just that much easier when you're not out their flailing on your own.

If you are a military member, veteran or the family of one and you don't know where to turn, there are resources out there for you.

(Canada) The Family Info Line (24/7)

1-800-866-4546

(Canada) The Member Assistance Program (24/7)

1-800-567-5803

(USA) Military OneSource (24/7)

1-800-273-8255 and Press 1

(England) Combat Stress (24/7)

0800-138-1619

(Australia) National Welfare Coordination Center (24/7)

1800-801-026

Remember, seeking help is not a sign of weakness. It is the strongest thing you can do for yourself and those who love you.

About the author

All The Way Home is the debut novel for writer Kim Mills, the author of the Canadian military family blog She is Fierce. Kim has been married to her high school sweetheart for over 15 years and together they have 3 children. You can find the five of them, along with their dog Trooper, at home wherever the army sends them.

Matt and Sarah's story

Carry Me Home

Available Spring, 2017

You can find Kim on social media:

Facebook
Facebook.com/sheisfiercecanada

Twitter
Twitter.com/reccewife

On the web
www.sheisfierce.net

23502473R00120

Made in the USA
San Bernardino, CA
26 January 2019